Donato Cascione

Tales from the Museum

Copyright © 2005, 2021 Donato Cascione

All rights reserved.

ISBN: 1500784249
ISBN-13: 978-1500784249

Foreword

They came from other parts, from far away, to recount through their eyes, which are in no way our eyes, what our rural culture was. By that we do not intend to misjudge them – more so after all the time that has passed since their arrival in Basilicata – if we maintain that their view was, however, too "external" compared with ours. It is true that they produced literary masterpieces and important scientific analyses but, in their academic and detached writings about the facts, they showed a lack of the human touch and depth of feeling towards those events – that had a social, economic and cultural nature as well as an artistic and anthropological one – that characterised the post-war years and the times of reconstruction to begin with and the land reform later, all over the South of Italy.

Donato Cascione, with his latest literary work (different from the others – sometimes "transgressive" – that we were accustomed to have from him during the seventies) sets it all in order. Now he shows us the reality of a peasant's life, both with the awareness of the inevitability of historical processes (which is typical of the Spencerian evolutionalist) and with, if you like, that necessary degree of materialistic pragmatism (that recalls the Haeckellian positivist thought) but also with the determination and cultural pride of one who is capable of regarding his own past in the critical spirit which is associated with the more recent dynamic vision of development of Ervin Lazlo.

Which corresponds, without doubt, to an act of conscience, but also to a denouncement from within of those cultural aberrations that during the 40s and 50s gave Basilicata the reputation of "amoral families" and of Weberian "disenchantment".

By way of a short digression from the theme, we cannot deny at this point that Ernesto De Martino and Annabella Rossi have bequeathed us a bitter and harsh view of Lucania, but indubitably analytic in the anthropological sense and without romantic literary embellishments (that risk "dressing-up" the authenticity of those recollections and emotions which differ from the exact nature of daily life).

Ernesto De Martino, with his studies and his travels around Basilicata, has "dug" – we might say – into the innermost parts of the "Lucana charm": between the sacred and the profane, magic and superstition. If his research is limited it is due exclusively to having viewed the reality of Lucania with too much detachment: with the typical attitude (which denotes his belonging to a cultural elite) of one who considers himself a depositary of academic knowledge.

Regarding that attitude, the artist Nini Ranaldi, who met Ernesto De Martino and accompanied him on his Lucanian excursions among the hills around Matera as well as the mountains of Potenza, recalled his excessively refined way of dressing (for example, his wearing kid-skin shoes, that contrasted violently to the necessity of living that experience from within).

The same thing happened with the writer Carlo Levi, the political exile in a region from which he understood how to gather all possible and imaginable contradictions (and thank God he did, no one would want it any other way), but who didn't know how to live from within for any length of time. And when he was eventually a free man and an MP, he could have dedicated his efforts constructively towards the development of this county. Whoever goes to Aliano today will surely find some old man or white-haired woman who will rebuke the Turin artist for all this.

In any case, he played his important part in this county: he accused the Italian government, declared "Matera is anarchy compared to Rome" and demonstrated his personality as an intellectual outside the regime and the city-hall logic. History today must recognise both sides: his failure on one hand and his efforts on the other. If there is a problem, a big problem, regarding Carlo Levi that must now be revealed – in order to analyse it critically and to surmount it culturally – it is that of the "organic intellectuals" who during the 60s and 70s wanted to emphasise their political ideas exaggeratedly: thereby dwelling too long on positions that were certainly interesting but not completely autonomous nor purporting an indigenous representation.

It is for this reason that an authentic rural culture, fascinating as it may be, but full of contradictions on the economic and social levels, gave birth to a false agricultural and pastoral civilisation: in fact one that has never existed within a framework of a welfare state or in other words a social well-being.

At this point we must acknowledge the writer and poet Donato Cascione, who is also a researcher that has found numerous ancient utensils and furnishings (so many that he has constructed a museum around them in the Sasso Barisano of Matera), and who has set this complex artistic and cultural affair, that belonged to people like Levi and De Martino, in order. He managed to do so by demonstrating an entropic dimension of an understanding of the facts, after having for years tried to discover the deepest truths, not the superficial ones, in the peasant existence. He did it by "digging down" into his roots, collecting everything possible regarding furnishings and various remains as well as memories and images. All this with the aim to interpret and better to understand that dimension of the land which belongs more and more to memory and less, much less, to the normal everyday life.

Today, by the use poetry in free and alternate rhymes, and tales with short paragraphs, Donato Cascione tells us about a world that doesn't exist any longer. To do so he employs his "third inner eye" that he refined during his years of literary militancy in experimental writing (which led him to publish with the editor Lacaita) and in his visual poetry (of which he was the pioneer in Basilicata). Thus he narrates, in these latest stories of his, a world full of contradictions on economic and social levels but rich in human interest too.

A world that must continue to exist in the form of a cultural archetype which could help us to create a new conscience (ecological if possible) and a new culture (of an anthropic nature). One outcome of this cultural operation of Donato Cascione will undoubtedly be a reflection on the dialogic sense of modern culture, and a proposal, a very strong one, to heighten our memory and creativity (that originate from our imagination and our feelings).

Thank you, Donato, for having in this way managed to empower creativity and to exalt a people, the country folks that have been emarginated up to now by a civilisation that prefers to praise the values of capitalism rather than the values of believing and sharing in genuine mutual respect.

Your social model, based on the exaltation of sentiments and on simplicity, is one in which we all must believe most sincerely in order to advance and better ourselves. And your words, your ideas, make a real contribution to that revolution from below that will change our present society into a world in which, in the words of the Prophet of the universal religion "the world is one country and humanity its citizens".

RINO CARDONE

Objects, memories and tales

The Museum-workshop of Donato Cascione, set up in some restructured rooms of a house with a small yard in the Sasso Barisano, appears to one that enters it as a place of memory which recalls life as it was in the Sassi before the Law 619 of 1952, which caused the evacuation of thousands of men and women resident there until then, sowed the seeds for turning it into a symbol of the peasant past that would become in time an object of aesthetic contemplation.

And if today the two rocky quarters are increasingly represented as the distinctive sign and the exportable logo of the town of Matera, world heritage and constant destination of tourists from all over the world, for those who spent there important periods of their lives they are places which evoke both affection and sufferings, signs of economic instability and of social and human solidarity, the context of childhood games and of the first apprenticeship, an evocative place of their existential conditions, now far gone and irretrievable in a residential dimension. For all of these people, especially the older ones, returning to the Sassi means to plunge again into a world existing no more, lost in their memory and re-emerging at the sight of the steep alleyways wedged between the lamioni and the cave-houses, between the churches built out of the tufo and what remains of the old bread baking ovens, the taverns and the workshops, around which was organised the social life of men and women, condemned to a low level of life and soon aged by privations, malnutrition and illnesses.

Of that life, led on the edge of survival, in conditions of extreme poverty and marginalization, Cascione's collection preserves traces and testimonies able to call forth strong emotions in those who, on entering, looking at and shyly touching the displayed artefacts, recall their use, their symbolic meanings, affective values, calling back to memory their own past conditions and enabling the generation of stories concerning objects that are revealed not as cold finds of a far and outdated history but warm autobiographical fragments of lives at times hopeless, capable of forming again a link with the past and to project it into the future.

Donato Cascione had the good idea of gathering some of those tales together, those which appeared to him more significant for a memorial representation and for their expressive incisiveness, reworking and presenting them in a form of writing in which the search for neatness of style does not at all compromise the immediacy and liveliness of the story, the emotive recollection of the recounted events, the will to communicate to generate a testimony and to hand down messages. And in mediating the recounting, Cascione gives a deep meaning to his work as a collector and museographer, establishing connections between the uncertain and at times chaotic present of the Sassi and their peasant and artisan past, a past that today induces silence and reflection and which calls forth emotion and respect at the thought of the price paid by generations of people, in that building and environmental context which has become, in time, a source of wonder and strong fascination for visitors from faraway lands and times, struck in their imagination by that extraordinary and charming agglomerate of forms which presents itself all of a sudden to eyes, unaware and often altogether oblivious of the inner significance of that sight.

Thus the objects gathered together and preserved in Donato Cascione's Museum-workshop of the peasant culture appear as living and tangible testimonies of those generations, of which, even through the tales they manage to generate reactivating their memory, demonstrate their capacity to interpret feelings and values, ways of behaviour and lifestyles, views of the world and hopes for a better future, with the effect of being able to offer to the current generation a contradictory vision of past worlds and at the same time of other possible and conceivable ones, even if deeply distant and different from them.

FERDINANDO MIRIZZI

Author's note

In 1998 I decided to do something constructive about the almost obsessive collection of tools and pieces of furniture of our Rural Culture that I had been forming over thirty-odd years, to the incredulity, the scepticism and, more often, the diffidence of those who knew me.

Encouraged by the tendency, rather diffused everywhere in the past few years, to give greater appreciation to this page in our recent history (so far treated with unjustified condescension by the official culture as the history of the subordinate classes), I reached the decision to create in this very place, the heart of the Sassi, a type of museum which would give our old town a greater expressive force.

Although at the planning stages there were many doubts and uncertainties on the way the itinerary should be arranged for the visitors, some points became immediately clear to me: the Museum had to belong to everybody, a vivacious place, somewhere in which this culture could be assembled and elaborated, provided with manifold structures that would permit their fruition on several levels and ample potential for information.

Furthermore, the first to enjoy these offerings should be the young people of Matera, who know so little about the way of life, be it in a social or economic context or within the family, of the generation before theirs. This is due to a form of rejection from the mind of that period (by those who experienced it) together with the burden of suffering that was an integral part of it; the result is, obviously, an interruption in the handing down of traditional customs and uses to the new generations.

I felt sure of the wonder and admiration of the tourists, and the interest and curiosity of the young people of Matera. But I wondered what would be the reaction of their grandparents who had spent their childhood and adolescence in the Sassi and, in some cases, even a longer time. Well, the reactions were varied and went from one extreme to the other: from rejection to reverence.

One old woman, over eighty years old, accompanied by her grandchildren and great-grandchildren, came one day but could not bring herself to cross the threshold of the Museum: she could not stand darkness and dampness and nothing I said about the reconstruction work done on the place could reassure her. Another woman, on the contrary, asked if she might stay all afternoon sitting in an environment so similar to that in which she spent her youth. She had never been as happy anywhere else.

Between these two extremes there is an increasing number of old people who show that they have come to terms in a balanced and serene way with their past, recognising many ethical values in it without missing the privations, the hard work and the suffering. These are the very same people who, during their visits, let themselves revive old memories. Their narratives never fail to amaze me and they manage to amplify and strengthen the cultural message of the exhibits in the Museum: everything becomes more human and thus more authentic and significant.

At first I only exhibited in the Museum those tales that struck me in a particular way. However, the requests of many visitors (above all tourists, emigrants from Matera or their descendants, students) drove me to publish a collection of these tales. This work, too, raised many doubts. Should I intervene decisively in the style of the narration, making it impeccable yet thereby robbing it of its intrinsic expressive connotations? Should I censure references to political responsibilities or to the clergy that were passed on to me not by experts in politics or religion but by "normal" people like me, who had experienced feelings that I now shared and regarding whose genuineness no one had the right to advance any doubts?

In the end I decided to respect as much as possible my interlocutors: you will find frequent pauses in the stories, due to the emotion of the moment; digressions that do not irritate but add to the story in some way; the recurring final considerations that some will certainly find rhetorical, but which should be interpreted as an attempt, on the part of the story-teller, to define the complexity of sentiments, sometimes contradictory, felt during the interview.

I have intervened only where necessary to fill in the gaps left where my visitors could not find the right words for certain strong feelings which were nevertheless shown by their facial expressions and unmistakable gestures.

Over the last twenty years, I told myself, experts of all kinds (sociologists, anthropologists, historians, architects, academics, etc.) have made the Sassi of Matera the central theme of their research and have issued all sorts of publications. But how often have they interviewed those who have lived there? It is only right and just that their voices complete the panorama formed by all the facets that make up the recent history of our town.

DONATO CASCIONE

Author's note to the second edition

This second edition, enriched with new poems, tales and images, has been published in response to the unexpectedly wide interest manifested towards this collection of chronicles by many and varied readers (many of whom foreigners).

The uncertainty of our current times urges us to strengthen our roots: ancient beliefs, validated by centuries of history and traditions, become irrefutable fixed points which support the truth, favour equanimity and give one hope for a dignified life.

It is possible to draw from the past the necessary strength to build a future on a human scale, free from false regrets and self-pity, and to avoid laying the blame on others.

DONATO CASCIONE

Author's notes to the third edition

The second edition has encountered as the first the favour of numerous readers, many of who were visitors of the Museum, who saw the publication as a complement to the Museum path effective in deepen the knowledge of the Sassi history.

That's why I prepared this third edition, enriched with new testimonies, verses, pictures, thoughts. It will be the last. I think that the collected material is sufficient to know and revisit our past and think about it.

What can we save and recover? Which were the wrong choices to be not repeated? Which aspect can be taken as a basis to plan our future? How this impressive amount of rational and emotional elements in our individual and social growth have to be managed, and in which direction?

I leave it up to readers to formulate wise answers to these pressing questions.

DONATO CASCIONE

ENTRY OF PALAZZO BARBERIS, HOUSE OF THE MUSEUM

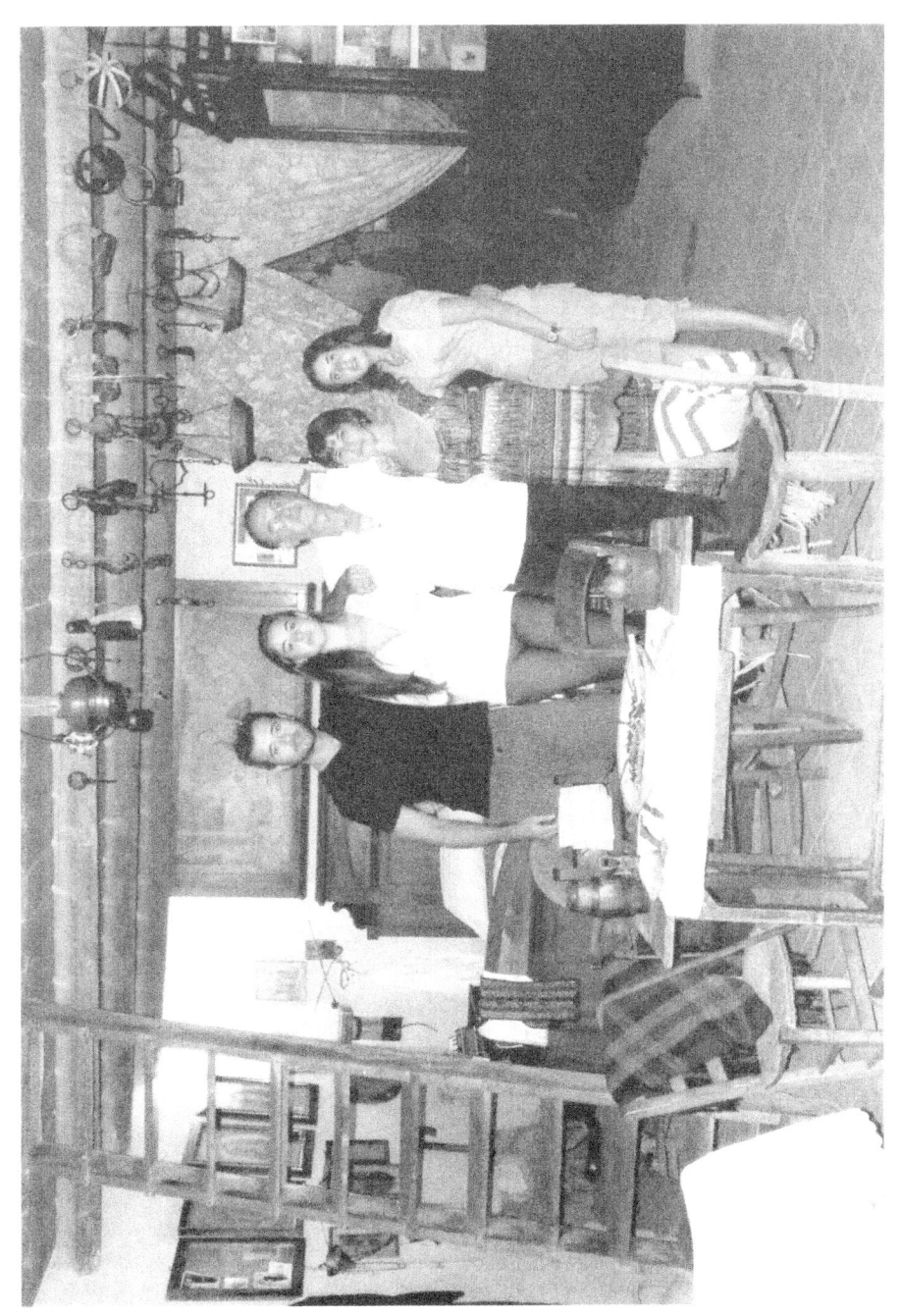

CASCIONE FAMILY INSIDE THE MUSEUM

The reasons for this Museum

Among the smells of sawdust, of stables, of ovens,
Of wine and oregano I grew up:
In the dust of the bricklayer's work
And the chatter of the gypsies, bartering horses.

I can still hear the sound of the carpenter's plane,
Of the hammer on the anvil, the screech of the cart brakes,
The swish of wheat falling into the grain chests,
The panting of the donkey exhausted by the farm work,
The desperate weeping over the death of a mule,
The song of the peasant woman as she kneads the dough,
The laughter over little things, faraway voices...

All this has been my world, yours too.
All this has built our future:
The identity of a people.

The shepherd boy
(story of Nicola A., 81 years old)

I lost both my parents when I was ten. My old grandmother sent me to the man in charge of a farm ten kilometres away from Matera, so that I could learn a trade.

A shepherd's job was very hard but the shepherds were even harder in their treatment of us boys. We had to watch over the flocks while they were grazing, so that they were not stolen or attacked by wolves; but the real work started at dawn when the animals were milked, the stalls cleaned out, the ricotta and other cheeses prepared, and the shearing carried out.

The shepherds, whether for the solitary life and lack of women or, having spent so much time in the company of animals they had begun to resemble them, had no pity for me nor for the other two boys from Altamura.

They shouted at us as soon as work commenced: their version of 'good morning' was "son of a ..., haven't you watered the animals yet?". In order to do that we had to draw water from the well in a bucket attached to a chain that unwound from a piece of wood that terminated in a type of ship's wheel, called the "macegna". We had to carry dozens of buckets of water from the well to the stalls. If, during the milking, due to a draught or something, a piece of hay or wood fell into the milk that was intended for cheese-making, the headman would become furious and beat us boys.

The owners of the farm never interfered in the administration of the labourers: they trusted blindly the headmen and gave them the responsibility of coordinating the work of the shepherds, the boys and the other farm labourers. Even when, in desperation, we wept piteously they ignored us: they had never heard nor taken notice of us. And yet they had children of our age: we saw them occasionally when they looked out of the windows of the farmhouse. We hated them too.

One day the headman sent me to Matera to fetch some oil and other provisions. Incidentally, we shepherd boys did not have any shoes and our clothes consisted in a pair of shorts and a chequered shirt. When the stink of our clothes became unbearable the headman yelled at us to wash ourselves more often. But we didn't have much time for that.

And so, after I had crossed various streams, taken short-cuts, climbed rugged hills and slithered down steep drops, I reached Matera at last with bleeding feet.

The owner's housekeeper, who lived under the master rooms, felt sorry for me and gave me a pair of shoes. They were broken and a few sizes too big but I was so delighted with them that I embraced the housekeeper. I took up my burden of provisions and, without stopping to rest, I set off on the return journey. On the way I had to sit down quite often as my feet were aching and thus, somehow, I fell into a deep sleep.

When I awoke I realised that someone had stolen the provisions. I was frightened to death at the thought of going back to the farm empty-handed. Everyone was waiting for me, not because I mattered to them but because they desperately needed the provisions.

When I told my story to the shepherds they beat me until the blood ran and then dragged me behind the boundary wall; there I was literally cast into a hole, a disused well more than three metres deep. I was left there for two days with nothing to eat or drink: nobody listened to my cries...

The years went by and changes took place in the farm. I became an expert shepherd and when the headman died, the new owner asked me to take his place. I married and had three children who now live in Milan...

A thousand memories and sufferings are hidden in these wooden tools, in these copper and iron utensils, in those carved sticks and sheep skins...

Nowadays you can hardly believe in these stories of such hard life, but they really did happen, my son.

Inside the Museum: shepherd's object

INSIDE THE MUSEUM: THE TRANSMISSION OF MEMORY

The brazier
(story of Maria C., 85 years old)

"I once burnt my foot in a brazier" said old Maria, catching sight of one near the entrance to the museum". I still have the scar.

It was a winter night and we were all gathered around the fire, five or six of us. It was almost dark and the cold was biting. We were waiting for my father to come with the laden mule, before we could have our dinner and go to bed.

Our grandmother told us stories of olden times, stirring the embers with a small shovel from time to time, so as to cook some potatoes. But there weren't many embers...

"Grandma, how long before we can eat?" we kept asking impatiently. "Hold out a little longer and we'll all eat together, at the right moment. Now I'll tell you another story so you'll not think about your hunger and tiredness..."

The wailing of tiredness

"It's the wailing of tiredness,
says the old woman, as she rocks the baby
Wailing, wailing,
you'll cry yourself to sleep, my son"

"Desperately crying in the cradle!
Has the baby eaten?"

"It's the wailing of tiredness, goodwife Nannina".
"He has spat out the cloth teat
soaked in sugar!"

"It's the wailing of tiredness, goodwife Nannina,
May Christ protect him and Our Lady bless him".
"The baby in the cradle
cries no more!"

"He has fallen asleep, like an angel".

Pucc d suunn
(translation in the Materan dialect by Giuseppe Leo Sabino)

"Jaè pucc d suunn
d'sh la vecchj ca annacaesh u nunn
chiangionn chiangionn
T'had add'rmaesc, fugghj m'j".

"Chiong d'sp'reet jund la neech!
Ho mangeet u criatyr?"

"Jae· pucc d suunn, ch'mma Nann'n"

"Ho sh'ttect u ciccet d pezz chjn d zìcch'r!"
"Jae· pucc d suunn, ch'mma Nann'n"
Crust u word i la Madenn u b'nd'sh".

U nunn nan chiong chjr
Jund a la neech!"
"S'hi add'rmiscyt prept com a n'ang'lucchj".

INSIDE THE MUSEUM: BARBERSHOP

INSIDE THE MUSEUM: PARTICULAR OF THE TYPICAL HOUSE

When even the calls of nature meant hard work...
(story of Immacolata S., 75 years old)

"When you go along memory's path, everything seems softened, misty; the images become vague, blurred: it is a security valve that lessens the pain. Then it even becomes enjoyable to talk about the past, because the flood in which we were drowning is behind us...

Early in the morning, like a thief, dressed in those few rags that I had, I used to creep through the streets of the Sassi clutching the chamber-pot (in spite of the wooden lid the smell would make me retch).

The ungrateful task of emptying the night soil into the sewer drain was usually assigned to women older than me. Unfortunately my mother had been ill for months and we all had to lift her bodily off the bed so as to look after her needs. For that reason my father had "ordered" me to do the job.

God knows how ashamed I felt every day when I had to do this task. The worst part was cleaning out the pot with the little water available.

My grandmother used to tell me that in many parts of the Sassi there wasn't a drain. Every morning at dawn the trumpet would sound to announce the arrival of the "carrizza", a cart with squeaking wheels and a huge wooden barrel. The human waste was thus collected every day from house to house and then spread on the fields as fertilizer...".

The cart builder
(story of Antonio F., 73 years old)

My father built carts all his life and he died of a heart attack while still in his workshop. It was a hard job that, however rough it may have seemed, required extreme precision, above all when making the wheels.

I can remember stacks of beech-wood in the shed: the planks were piled on top of each other in a fresh ventilated place so that they would season uniformly.

If you wanted to make a wheel you had first to determine the diameter: those for carts were 1,60cm across while the barrow wheels (used to transport wood, stones, etc.) measured 80cm in diameter. The first part to be made was the hub, that was generally 40cm long: this involved hewing out and turning the wood, making holes for the spokes and then securing the lot with four iron rings, to prevent any splintering caused by compression. To finish with a central hole was carved out for the axle.

Then came the preparation of the spokes: twelve spokes of 65cm and six semi-circles for the circumference, fashioned with the help of large wooden compasses. The mounting of the outer iron rim was the last part of the job: a blacksmith came to the workshop and used a length of string to measure the circumference of the wheel and then made a copy in iron. At three o'clock in the morning a fire was lit right round each rim which very soon became red-hot and expanded.

At this point the blacksmith (helped by at least three people) fitted them round the wheels, hammering them into place. Immediately after that the iron was doused with several bucketfuls of water to make it adhere to the wood as it cooled. The iron rims were further secured to the wheels by six nails so that they would remain fast during the wear and tear of time. Sometimes, if the blacksmith had not measured them correctly, the wheels did not fit the red-hot iron rims perfectly: when that happened foul language was rife because there was the risk that delivery would be late.

It was on one such occasion that my father, infuriated, threw a spanner at me. I had arrived late to give him a hand. I still have the scar on my forehead. But I have never borne him a grudge for it: deep down I deserved it, for other reasons too.

The master craftsmen were very severe with the apprentices, including their own sons, because they maintained that work is a serious business and paying customers should be served with honesty.

I worked with my father for many years and I studied in the evenings. I know all the secrets of this trade, which was also my grandfather's.

INSIDE THE MUSEUM: CART BUILDER'S SHOP

The donkey

The old donkey, when it falls,
makes a noise:
it's the thud of its weary bones.
It sounds like pots
overturned by fidgety children.
It appears to laugh,
as it has never laughed before during its life:
and so it lies there,
like a magnificent statue,
sneering at death,
even as the dust
blinds it.

U cidd
(translation in the Materan dialect by Giuseppe Leo Sabino)

U cidd vecchj, quonn ciamb'caesh,
feesh r'maour;
jaht u ndimm d l'èss'r app'sand't:
porn a b'dae sartòsh'n
m's cap'saoutt da wagnyn tandavudd.
Peer a b'daè ca r'r,
com na ho r'ryt mej n-v'ta saouj:
i dax' r'manaesh,
com a na stotuw d morm,
pugghj p fess la mert,
mendr la paouvl
no feesh v' daé nidda chj'.

The grain chest
(story of Teresa S., 65 years old)

It was terribly hot when we started looking for little Maria: it was the middle of August. Some were barefoot and swore when they trod on the hot cobbles.

We called her name for hours as we searched the numerous paths and the houses built one on top of the other. Nothing. No one had seen her.

We feared she may have fallen down the steep bank where a muddy stream run. Somebody else thought she may have gone into the town as she had asked for permission to do so at times. Still nothing.

Our mother had seen her playing with a rag ball by the front door. Then, in the time needed to collect the ball, she had vanished!

Our old grandmother was having a nap in the shade of an archway. As soon as she woke up she joined in the search to her best ability, questioning the neighbours. Then she had a sudden intuition. No one had looked in the grain chest.

We all gathered round as the lid was raised, and there was our darling. She was asleep, stretched out on the grain.

INSIDE THE MUSEUM: THE GRAIN CHEST

INSIDE THE MUSEUM: PARTICULAR OF THE TYPICAL HOUSE

Giuseppe
(story of Pasquale C., 89 years old)

One winter's evening my father brought home Giuseppe huddled up on the saddle of the mule and wrapped in a woollen blanket. He was no more that twelve years old. No one has ever forgotten that evening. It was in 1930.

"Everybody hurry up and come here!" cried my father at the door. We went to him in the dark, took our little brother from the back of the mule and laid him out on the bed. Our grandmother lit a petrol lamp and looked at the boy. She place her bony fingers on his forehead and said: "My son, there's nothing you can do for Giuseppe: his body is already cold".

Our father approached the bed slowly and held the dying boy in his arms: "Peppino, you told me that your knees were shaky and you had a temperature, but you were dying, curled up beside the wheel of the cart. What a wretched life we have... We are born and die like animals!"

We had never heard him talk like that: he spoke little, as little as possible. His talk was reduced to the bare minimum like the needs of our life: oil for the lamp, flour, pulses, water and only the most essential clothing.

Our worst misfortune was the loss of our mother: she had died in childbirth, leaving seven children. I was the oldest and I was only sixteen. It was up to me to take care of my brothers and sisters. Our grandmother, as far as she could and for the little that she could see, helped me to keep the house tidy, which only consisted in a large room and a stall. That evening the officer of the law was called and came after a couple of hours. A doctor came too, old with gold-rimmed spectacles. "He has died of illness" said the doctor. He wrote out the certificate and they left. In those days it was easy to die of illness.

They had made a habit of lying. The truth was that children died of privations, of malnutrition and overwork. No one protected them, no one took care of them; there was never the time nor the means to defend them from a cruel death, from the indifference of the times and from man himself.

How thin Giuseppe was! He looked like a bunch of wheat, blond and straight. That same evening we dressed him... Dressed... is one way of saying it: a pair of dark patched shorts, cut from an old cloak of our grandfather, and a ragged singlet. We would have done better to bury him wrapped in a linen sheet, like Jesus Christ was.

Very soon the neighbours started to arrive: silently they offered us their condolences and then wept together. It was their way of showing solidarity with us, not least for the absence of our mother. Our father stood by the door throughout, sometimes gazing into space, other times at the dead child on the bed, or the mule that, as a member of the family, stood at the back of the stall, silently like the others.

The next morning the priest came to give the extreme unction: he did not utter a single comforting word to anyone. His duty done, he left without a glance at anyone... but he made sure he looked at us when, at Easter, he came to bless the house and our father donated whatever he could: eggs, a chicken, a little wheat.

Early that afternoon they took away the coffin, to our unbearable grief. I still remember it, after nearly seventy years, as though it were today.

The next day, at dawn, our father took the mule and started out for the fields. Life had to go on.

The death of children

The death of children didn't make history,
or it made it for others.
Missing from the cemeteries,
heaped up in communal pits,
without any imagery:
They only had one when they were dying,
On a straw bed,
With torn shorts and poor rags on.

There has been more deaths in the Sassi
Than stars in a night sky
And grains in a wheat field...
Who will talk about them? Some cold statistic
Will banish them to the lines of a history book.
Let's not feel guilty, though:
This has been the price too.

INSIDE THE MUSEUM: SCALPELLINO'S SHOP

INSIDE THE MUSEUM: POTTER'S SHOP

The dead at home
(story of Francesco P. C., 76 years old)

I almost pleaded for him to come in. He continued to stand there, peeping in as though he heard a voice from the past or was looking for someone or something. He was looking for both as this unbreakable duality belonged to his past. Eventually he made his decision and crossed the threshold. He seemed to me uncertain, shy in spite of his advanced age.

The house he was visiting rendered him wordless and the objects that he looked at with apparent detachment conveyed his thoughts far, far away. And I respected this, his reliving his past, I avoided any interruption of his journey among his memories by not greeting him at all.

After a while he came back to the present: the wrinkles on his face softened as he spoke to me. "I'd like you to know that I was born in this house and before me my father and my grandfather and before my grandfather our history is lost in the mist of time. It was a hard life, very hard even though there were happy times, marked by simplicity and dignity... What frightened me most when I was a child wasn't the presence of the animals inside the house but that of the dead people. Yes, the dead people at home.

Prior to 1800 (when the cemetery in Via IV Novembre was created), the dead were buried in the church, and the priests and monks in the underground part of the church, sitting in niches carved out of the rock. The poor souls' bones were kept in collective ossuaries. The difference between us and them was always present: superior (or so they considered themselves) even in death. Those who couldn't afford an ossuary for financial reasons or because they had been interdict for other motives (for not having donated enough to the church, for bad relations with the clergy or for having led a life that didn't adhere to the civil and moral tenets), those people were buried in the house, in a cavity similar to the well from which we used to draw water...

Once something happened that upset me badly... My father had never opened that trapdoor, neither had I nor my brothers. My grandfather, due to some household repairs, was obliged to do so and I remember that he sent us all out in the country... When we returned he made no mention of what had happened, nor the day after or ever.

All that I have told you is true" said my nameless friend "In our thousand year history anything can be found, if you care to search for what you want. The best lymph comes from the roots of our ancestors, who leave their mark in no small way throughout our lives".

Sometimes I too think about that trapdoor, about the bodies accumulated there over the centuries, about this unpleasant legacy that fell on my shoulders, about the sound of mules' hooves and the nailed boots of the farm workers that passed upon it, about the heavy tread of the sandals of visitors, the tapping of the heels of tall tourists who explore the museum from end to end with a puzzled air, looking at me as though I were a Martian just arrived on Earth.

The cavapozzi (The well digger)

I can hear you without seeing you.
You are digging the well according to orders,
in the little light of the candle.
You are more alone than you would think...
The sound of the pickaxe dulls the heart.
May your breath not run out,
may your courage not leave you!...

There's always someone or something
digging inside us, day and night:
the wind lifts the dust
and scatters it everywhere.

The seamstresses
(story of Angela and Anna M., 70 and 73 years old)

"My mother and my grandmother were seamstresses" one of the two polite women confided looking at me in the eyes, as they stood beside the dressmaking table reconstructed in the museum. She has a slight Piemontese accent. But their apparent northern origins are quickly shown up as misleading by their use of some Materan terms that I have rarely heard.

"We emigrated in the 60s with all the family because we were tired of so much privation. Taken on by a large tailoring concern, we soon demonstrated that we were not afraid of hard work. The proprietor quickly understood that we were very competent and in no time the customers started to ask expressly for us, thanks to the dedication we gave to our work. For this reason he held us in great esteem and paid us punctually.

I remember when we used to live in Matera, for the occasion of the local saint's day, crowds of people came to our house in Via Muro to order their suits, skirts, shirts and bodices. That was the only period of intense work... Then, suddenly, the orders were fewer: just odd garments to be changed or turned. An overcoat to be transformed into shorts... a coat to be shortened...

Before the celebration of the 'Madonna della Bruna' the women would bring us their materials, and after taking their measurements we would start work. We scarcely stopped until we ironed the completed article, using the box-irons filled with coal-embers.

At home we all worked: my mother, my grandmother and we girls of fifteen and seventeen years. We continued to sew until late at night.

At three o'clock sharp in the morning, our grandmother woke our mother and us up. "Grandma's beauties" she would say "wake up. The fete is approaching and our customers are anxious!". She heated some malted milk for us and then straight to work.

If one of them was short of money she could pay with some olive-oil, flour or other commodity... We managed anyway. If we were summoned by some grand lady we were delighted, as we could be paid more... But it didn't happen very often.

So, as I said, we moved to the North and after a few years of working for others, we set up on our own. And it didn't go at all badly. Today our children are highly appreciated and well paid fashion designers. After nearly half a century we're not sorry that we worked so hard, went without sleep and many other things, in our pride of having built a future for someone".

Inside the Museum: tailor's shop

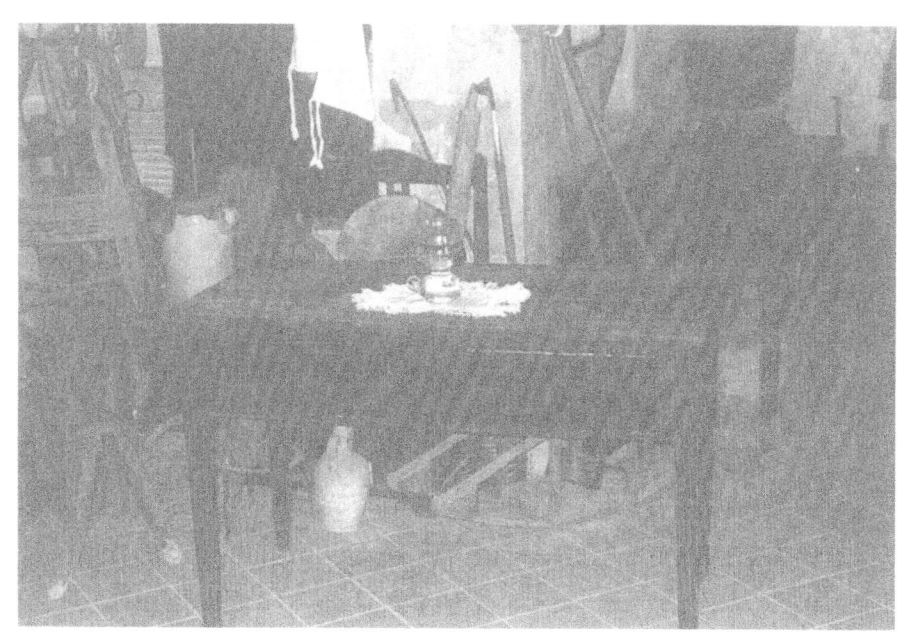

OIL LAMP, HALF OF XIX CENT.

The mouse
(story of Giuseppe L., 84 years old)

At the end of the nineteenth century the houses were lit by petrol or oil lamps, or by lanterns made of brass, clay or tin. There were beautiful lamps in the homes of the masters, in hand-painted opaline, with glass funnels and a switch to regulate the flame near the wick.

The poorest people, like us, had a lamp too, if it can be considered one, in its simplest form: a beaker full of water with a film of oil floating on top and in the middle a wick-holder. The latter was a cardboard disc about the size of a fingernail with the waxed wick in the centre, measuring about 3cm. The illumination it gave was very faint and each room had one, or one was taken from room to room. Times were hard and we had to economize where possible.

Once, we noticed that the little light burned away faster than usual over a few days: usually a glass of oil, thanks to the greatest possible care being taken, lasted more than fifteen days, since it was lit only for a short while in the evening, while we had dinner, did some odd jobs and then... everybody to bed.

This fact made my mother suspicious, as she was always so careful to make ends meet. So, after having put us all to bed, one on a bench, others on the mezzanine, some in the big bed and even someone in a drawer, she filled to the brim the lamp, which she had extinguished a few minutes before. Then she lay down on the huge bed, filled with maize leaves where two of my little brothers were already sleeping.

The next morning she woke up early and hurried to check on the level of the oil. I remember her expression of annoyance as she looked at the beaker.

For the entire day she worked around the house, without saying a word to anyone about what had happened. And neither did we say anything, for fear of being implicated in spite of being innocent.

The following night all was revealed to her. As soon as we children were under the bedclothes, she left her bed and squatted in a corner, where it was dark, to keep an eye on the beaker. She had to wait quite a long time watchful. Suddenly she heard a rustle from the chest of drawers: something was moving among the things piled on top of it. She crept closer and, to her great surprise, discovered a mouse licking the oil of the lamp.

In that way we were definitely exculpated.

The cavamonti (The rock digger)

I have chewed dust and spittle,
I have dug out with the pickaxe
"quadrelle, pedacche and catene"[1].
I looked like a white mole,
The dust itching my scalp
The sun baking my skin, burning my eyes.

I was a defenceless animal.
One day the pickaxe bent my back.
The "pezzetto lungo"[1] is still there,
An impressive architrave,
Intact, just as I extracted it:
It will still be there when I'll die.

---

[1] Quadrelle, pedacche, catene, pezzetto lungo are all differently sized tufo blocks.

SOUVENIR-PHOTO WITH A LITTLE PLASTER PIG

THE STRAIN

Filomena
(story of Nunzia F., 80 years old)

Not much was known about Filomena in the neighbourhood. No one could say where she was born or had lived in her youth. She had neither children nor relations. She lived alone in a cave-dwelling, the widow of a rope-maker who had died after a very few years of marriage.

She was very old but nobody knew how old. When she was asked her age she replied that she couldn't remember. She didn't remember anything unpleasant to her. She was extremely poor and lived thanks to the charity of people.

How many times my grandmother recounted to me stories about her when I was a child! She frequently sent me to take some soup or bread to her: "Take something to that poor soul!" she would say while she was spinning the wool. "Some people are even worse off than we are. Good works are the Christian's first duty".

So Filomena's life dragged on in this way, full of pain and almost always shut up in her cave. Those of the neighbourhood took care of her as though she was everybody's relative and because she did something for all of them. She handed out advice on the health of people and animals, she made good-luck charms from bits of cloth, she recited charms for falling in love and other things.

Her home was full of religious pictures always lit by candles and tapers. She never accepted money. She only wished to be loved by everyone.

She had remedies against ill-will or spells, for curing worms and dispelling fear, for children's fevers or stomach-aches: among her papers the correct formula could always be found to ward off all ills.

Even the problems of pregnant women she dealt with. She spent most of the day reciting the rosary, preferably in the dark. When we didn't hear from her for a few days, we were uncertain about what to do. Then we asked the men to break down her door. We found her dead, already in a state of decay. Her burial was paid for by the whole neighbourhood.

After a few years her house was taken over by a distant relative of her husband. Very soon strange things began to happen. During the night the bed sheets were jerked and some objects were found moved. The new owner decided to go to live elsewhere, in the fear that his pregnant wife could die of fright.

People started to say that the place was haunted so no one went to live there. Even today some old person remember this story, but will not willingly talk about it.

MATERAN PEASANT (1944)

> per far passare i vermi
> si dice il Lunedì Santo,
> Martedì Santo, Mercoledì Santo,
> Giovedì Santo, Venerdì Santo,
> Sabato Santo, e poi si dice al rovescio.
> Sabato Santo, Venerdì Santo, Giovedì Santo
> mercoledì Santo, Martedì Santo, Lunedì Santo
> Domenica Santa e Pasqua, e i vermi
> Sciaccia. La Notte di Natale fu
> una festa Principale.
> Bella è la Madre e più bello è
> il figlio, fai passare i vermi a
> questo figlio, recitare un paternostro
> ave e gloria padri

ANCIENT "THERAPEUTIC PRAYER"

per la Paura

Tre gloria padri a l'eterno Padre.
Paura dove vai, vado per la strada.
Paura a dove vai, vado in fronte a questa persona
non andare quella e carne battezata, alla
fonte e stata presa Pane benedetto a mangiato
aqua santa a bevuto, come chiudesti il fiume
di Giordano, così chiudi il ~~~~ cuore di questa
persona. Da in fronte ti prendo e in terra ti getto
Da in fronte ti prendo e in terra ti getto
Da in fronte ti prendo e in terra ti getto si dice 3
volte con la mano sulla fronte facendo segno di croce
col dito, e poi l'ostesso 3 volte con la mano sul petto
e dopo recitare un pater ave e gloria Padre

ANCIENT "THERAPEUTIC PRAYER"

per laffascia e Dolore di testa
Tre gloria padre al padre eterno. Affascia
Affascia dove vai, vado per la strada e
trovi avanti a Gesu e la vergine Maria.
Affascia dove vai, vado in fronte a
questa persona, non andare che quella
e come battezzato, dalla fonte sta presa, e
pane benedetto a mangiato, aqua santa
a bevuto, come chiuderti il fiume di
Giordano cosi chiudi il cuore di questa
persona. Da in fronte ti prendo e in
terra ti getto. Da in fronte ti prendo e
in terra ti getto. Da in fronte ti prendo
e in terra ti getto, questa si dice solo 3
volte solo in testa, e recitare
un paternostro e ave
gloria padri

Ancient "therapeutic prayer"

Once defeated, now triumphant
(story of Cosimo D.T., 78 years old)

The occupation of the land was the most right and natural thing we could do. Too many injustices endured had shaken off that torpor that had lasted for centuries, also called resignation.

It was historically necessary to relegate to oblivion the words "assignrì" (yes sir) and "salariato" (farm hand). It was a right due to us by history even before the master. And it wasn't painless; but in the end even we had something to treasure: the land. The land to work and to love.

That was the end of the farm hand's nightmare: too much hard work for too little pay. The master had enjoyed all the benefits.

The next chapter in the story of our efforts was the land reform. We had to work on the hard-earned land and make ends meet with the few implements we had: a plough and a mule. But nothing could make us go back to the life of a farm hand.

Some, for pride's sake, emigrated and abandoned the land or left it to a neighbouring farmer. They renounced for ever the fate of a peasant for that of a factory worker.

Nowadays, after so many years, when I wander along the paths of memory I recall it all and it gives me a strange and enjoyable feeling the fulfilment of a life. I have worked all my life and nothing has bowed me down, neither bad harvests nor death in the family. I have respected the essential values of the human race: religion, the family, work and a simple life.

This is the heritage I shall leave to my children: I hope and pray that they will know how to keep it safe and improve on it.

WEDDING IN 1940

THE MAN AND THE MULE

The man and the mule

There once was a time when man and mule were one,
one flesh,
one breath,
one single human adventure.
The animal, a member of the family,
was cared for and mourned
like one of the family.
The man put up with the smells of the animal
with which he shared the cave-dwelling.
They were bound by ties
mysterious and fateful, to say the least.
The woman, when they came home,
took care of the mule
speaking to it softly
calling it by name.
Sometimes she murmured in its ear,
after having dried the sweat on its body
and letting it stand before the entrance to the cave
for a while, so that the change in temperature
would do it no harm.
Then, after having spread sacks on the steep steps,
for fear of the mule slipping and falling,
she guided it with a tight rein to the back of the stall.
Nearly brushing it, the mule would pass by the table
where the woman had set
the enormous dish of *maccheroni* with oil and garlic,
eagerly eyed by the numerous family
who waited in silence, watching
as the ancient ritual was carried out.

A letter from Milan
(letter of Stefano D., 75 years old)

Dear friend,

Probably you will not remember me. It doesn't matter. I went to Matera some time ago and I visited the Sassi, my old home in the Barisano, restored and incorporated with other houses into your museum.

When you are seventy-five and you revisit scenes which formed part of a period of your life which was not very happy, it leaves a deep scar on your heart. It's impossible to describe: a storm of emotions and memories that tightens your throat and brings tears to your eyes.

In 1947, after the death of my mother, I went to Milan with my father and four brothers, in search of fortune. We all worked very hard and rarely returned to Matera. My father died after three years, perhaps due to homesickness: we scarcely ever talked... The weight of the passing years and the insistent thought of going back has made me feel melancholy. "I want to be buried in the cemetery of Matera" I always tell my children and I hope my wish will be fulfilled.

Your museum has caused me to relive my past of simple games, work in the fields, the neighbourhood where I used to live, the mule, the incredible hard work of my parents, the corpse of my mother on the high bed, the tears, the heat, the flies...

I remember, when I was a child, one day my mother was kneading the dough and singing in front of the house entrance. The early morning sun and the scent of sweet basil made her cheerful.

She had set me down inside the house, on a small chair with a hole in the seat under which there was a chamber-pot. I cried as hard as I could in order to attract her attention, but she didn't hear me. I felt a strong pain down below... At last, after quite a long time, my mother came running over to me in a fine fright: that cat had attempted, jumping up over and over again, to tear off my testicles! There were drops of blood in the chamber-pot.

With firm movement she washed me with the water from the *rizzola* (a terracotta vessel), then she called aunt Maria for the *astrumm* (the rite to dispel fear).

Dear friend, a visit down memory lane is always a tonic for the heart and the soul. Thank you for the courage you have shown in obliging us to recall that which is shortly to disappear forever.

MATERAN EMIGRANT

INSIDE THE MUSEUM: PARTICULAR OF THE WEAVING ROOM

Spindle spindle

"Spindle spindle,
spool spool..."
The old woman shatters in my heart
in thousand little silver pieces:
a fan of light
for my eyes too bright.
Her shadow is like a clot of blood
On lips of clay.

Her voice I hear again
if I listen carefully to the ancient sound
like a lullaby:
"Naked when born, naked when dead;
A rose in your hand
A coin in your mouth..."

"Spindle spindle,
spool spool..."
The old woman unravels the days
we live for better or worse,
winds them 'round the spinning wheel,
Squeaky as though tired.
The cold wool of regret,
the soft wool of sweet memories,
the prickly wool of conflicts,
the warm wool of love.

The new quarters
(story of Eustachio P., 80 years old)

Finally the longed-for gift arrived! Those gifts from the government to the socially underprivileged: those with pigs in the home and chickens and mules thrown in.

They were great yellow boxes, full of small and large apartments, for different sized families. We had waited for this moment for years.

The question of the Sassi had become important for the politicians during the electoral campaign. Everyone of them was ready to show great generosity in the hope of gaining a seat, at our expense.

Yet again, we were somebody's meal-ticket. Sometimes the poverty of some means the wealth of others.

But we had no interest in that business. First of all because we couldn't understand all that plotting and paperwork; secondly because our lives were made up of unending needs, of flocks of children, of backs aching from hard work, of poor harvests and getting drunk in the ciddaro (a wine-cellar bar) to forget.

In those days the homes in the Sassi were the national disgrace. Now they are inhabited by the children of those who turned up their noses at the mention of the Sassi. Everything has changed from the outside to the inside, from the walls to the hearts. Is there anymore sense in these houses without us? Is there any sense in modifying them according to the social status of those who will now live in them?

Once upon a time there was a brazier in every home and not much furniture. Nowadays you can see fur coats and dozens of clothes in walnut wardrobes in the style of Louis Whatshisname: it's history gone mad.

They bought us out for our hunger: the mirage of a better future, their trickery worked yet again. In that way our heritage was bartered away, the collapse of peasant tradition.

How proud we were when our names were mentioned in the long list of the needy! The voice emerged from the grey military loudspeaker and echoed all around the square. The assignment documents were handed out and we looked at each other with pride: we felt we were the most important people in the world. But not even on that day did we smile at each other, maybe out of an ancient sense of diffidence.

On the platform all the personages were present: from the mayor to the MP, from the sycophant dogsbody to the *carabiniere* all dressed up, with their painted wives, evidently sorry for all the troubles that a cruel fate had heaped upon our worthy heads. How many fine-sounding words were uttered that day! Their mouths overflowed with honey, but their speeches left no trace, not even the fragile vestige left by a snail.

But worse was yet to come. Having achieved their ends, they cheated us when the gifts were unwrapped: many accepted their new way of life, others didn't. We had to learn to think in terms of "condominium" and no longer of "neighbourhood".

A few of us went back to the old houses in the evenings because certain values essential to their lives were not to be found in the new quarters. In your old age you can't sustain radical changes; it isn't possible to wipe out all the past in one clean stroke.

The old folk couldn't sleep because they missed the breath of the mule on their necks which had been like a lullaby for them, the lullaby that their mothers had deprived them of. Therefore, so as not to create serious precedents, the entrances to all the old homes were bricked-up, leaving only a small space for letting air circulate.

In the new quarters there was no room for the mule or the donkey; the spaces beside the buildings were occupied by cars and lorries. The carts were abandoned in the country or out in the Sassi, where they had always been, and the animals sold. One or two continued to use them, leaving the carts and the animals in sheds outside the town every evening.

But it didn't last long. Our hearts were eaten up by nostalgia thanks to our forever recalling the past. And so we stopped talking about it, for fear of poisoning what was left of our lives. Distances had been greatly reduced: death was there mixed up with memories of our vineyards, of the burning heat of harvest time, in the wine-vats during grape-harvest. It was there sitting on the *chiancodda* (a small stool) and it held its wrinkled face in its bony hands, almost as though it was disconcerted by the prospect of bringing our lives to an end.

Our sons and daughters, who had been children when we brought them to the new quarters, settled down in this new environment: they found work, married and had their own children. Our grandchildren now have neither roots nor history: they question me about this or that.

In a few years, when the old guard will disappear altogether, the peasant tradition will be only a far-off memory, a rag of a confused dream that clouds our mind when we wake up. A story that will be of interest only to a few.

Someone might say: "Did we really live here? Did a mule pass through this room, where now there is a nice parquet or a fine stone floor, covered with many coloured rugs?"

A little while ago I was approached by a smart lady wearing a split skirt and expensive shoes: she smiled at me and invited me to see the house that she had had restructured. I did not take to her mauve-painted lips: my first thought was to get away as quickly as possible from that house that was mine no longer.

1955: Senator Emilio Colombo (President of the Committee on the Reclamation of the Sassi, at that time) assigns the first new housing (ph. Evangelista)

1955: ENTRANCE TO A HOUSE IN THE SASSO BARISANO IS WALLED-UP; SENATOR COLOMBO ATTENDS THE OPERATION (PH. EVANGELISTA)

The greys of my houses

Before I close my eyes,
long before, I want to store up, as an ant stores up,
the tones of grey in my mind's eye.
The greys of my houses
built with such skilled architecture by poor hands,
are not to be found on any palette.

Those greys
recall joys and sorrows
they savour of past centuries
which are our history.
Those greys, more vivid that ochre,
are inside us, only in us,
who are dreams and reality.

Where does that ancient stairway lead to?
"To the depth of truth" you told me.
We followed it with our hearts in our mouths,
all in one breath, as though we were still children.

The glass bell
(story of Antonietta M., 73 years old)

"Before we left the house of our ancestors – Antonietta shyly confided in me, standing beside the bed in the main room, below the mezzanine – we considered the furniture that would fit our new home. A great many ornaments were thrown away, other were exchanged with the ragmen. The dowry furniture (a chest of drawers, a wardrobe, a dressing-table) were sold. The glass-bell we donated to the Church of St. Anthony Abbot, to be placed on the altar.

Other neighbours of ours had the same idea. Very soon the altar was covered with glass bells containing figures of the Baby Jesus in wax or wood, the Madonna of Bruna or Our Lady of Sorrows, of saints of all sorts.

There was a desire to have a complete change, a stubborn determination to leave in the Sassi everything that had contributed to our growing old, to the memory of seeing our children being carried away, dead after even a minor ailment... By leaving our old homes we wanted to wipe the slate clean.

But when, after a few months, we moved into our long-dreamed of apartment (where we could finally wash ourselves in a comfortable bath-tub whenever we pleased, where we didn't have to fetch water from a well, where the floors weren't rough and ancient, where every type of worm or maggot brought out by dampness no longer existed for us) the past that we thought we had buried, having abandoned all those things and our Madonna, was still alive in our minds.

So I thought I would go and fetch my glass bell from St. Anthony church. But it wasn't there, all of them had gone... That day I felt particularly sad and lost.

I returned to the our old house, now empty, hoping to find something that had belonged to my mother, but there was nothing left!

Perhaps there will never be a time when we shall fully understand whether or not we had made a mistake! The bitter taste in my mouth will be with me always, until the day I die.

What idiocy to think we could tear out the past from our minds by throwing away our material possessions. What did our Madonna have to do with it? Maybe too often we had prayed to her to resolve our difficulties: from illness to fruitful harvests, from keeping the mule healthy to the health of our grandmother. And how many times had our prayers been answered?

But now I would enjoy dusting and loving the glass bell, if only for a religious respect of what it represents: it would pacify my soul while I await that sweet and definitive sleep that we all hope for at the end of our lives".

MADONNA OF BRUNA MADE IN TERRACOTTA

WATER SUPPLY (PH. GENOVESE)

The fountain of love
(story of Vincenzo A., 76 years old)

That Saturday there was a huge crowd around the fountain. It hadn't rained for months and the rain-collecting tanks carved out of the rock in our houses were dry and muddy.

The shrilling of the women of every age and of children, carrying clay vessels, tin buckets, bottles etc., was added to the noise of the tools of the craftsmen working in front of their shops.

Partly for the heat, partly for the irritability and that insidious malaise brought on by constant want, that so frequently provokes petty quarrels, apparently superficial (because the problem of ill-health was ever-present, and came out at the least provocation) biting words flew among us often. It was always that way with people who needed a scribe to do any work of request.

But we should have used our teeth elsewhere, in other places where, unknown to us, our fate was administered, the fate of ants stupefied by daily penury. Today we often use the word 'survive', but in those days it was "campé", making out.

Even the simplest things became complicated. Like that day at the fountain. After waiting for hours my turn arrived at last. But a girl slightly older than me pushed in. So, one word following another, a violent quarrel broke out which, some years later, led to a fine marriage and a numerous family.

But that day ended up with the girl breaking the *r'zzola* (a terracotta water vessel) on my shoulders; I threw my iron bucket at her while the onlookers laughed merrily. Later she also received two hard slaps from her mother, who lived nearby, on the higher grounds of the town...

In the days following this incident the first signs of falling in love became obvious between us. What can you do? Straight away I loved that strong character which has played such an important part in all the years we have spent together!

Those men

Those men didn't laugh
and they spoke only when necessary,
they were not gentle with their women:
they were incapable of giving a caress
or of speaking words of love.
Those men coupled on the high beds
the mattresses filled with maize leaves,
and they brought forth litters of barefoot children
when they were drunk or to avoid being killed by their rage.
Those men, silent shadows,
moved around like agitated ants,
surviving through all the misfortunes
that life had in store for them.
Those men had more than enough dignity.
Do not mistake it for contempt.
Today, in these houses in which, of those born,
two thirds would die of typhus, malaria or other diseases,
our vanity is celebrated.
Those men portrayed beside their mule,
a distilled picture of powerlessness and poverty,
are our "false pride",
sacred relics of a world
that belongs to us only as a commodity
or to satisfy our lack of roots.
Those men, if they came back to life,
would laugh heartily
at all the false sentiments
created around them.

Those men (ph. H. Cartier Bresson)

ANCESTORS OF THE AUTHOR (1913)

Harvest time
(story of A.D., 72 years old)

Very early in the morning we started out for the fields on the cart. When it was harvest time every member of the family gave a hand except for the old people who stayed at home.

Even small babies came, wrapped in woollen shawls, since there was no-one to look after them.

Once the implements were organized the work started early. In every field there were wild pear trees and the farm workers left their carts in their shade together with the few things they had brought with them, and the gourds full of water so that they didn't become too warm; everybody ate their food together.

While my brothers, sisters and parents worked in the fields, my baby sister slept in a cradle made out of a blanket tied at each end and hung on the branch of a tree.

Every so often I gave it a push to make it rock and then I returned to the wheat. The baby, to tell the truth, cried a lot due to the excessive heat and I, only six years old at that time, had to watch over her so as to call the others if necessary.

But it was hard for me to stay still: I was too fascinated by the mule drawn reaper at work. I followed it through the corn-stalks, which scratched my legs, but I couldn't keep up with the mules so I was left behind all alone and I began to cry suffering from the heat. "I'm too hot" I said "I'm too hot!".

My mother, in order to console and distract me, suggested that I went to my aunt who was working in the next field and ask her if it was just as hot there.

My mother's sister, whose field was even hotter, because there were so few crops that she couldn't even feed her children (in fact, some years later she emigrated to Canada), replied with a kind smile: "As it is there so it is here".

The tragedy
(story of E.C., 85 years old)

They had just finished building the road that runs from the Sassi to the modern part of town. We said goodbye to the mule-tracks, the open drains, the precipices along the gorge. The stone bridges (that connected one part of the Sassi to the other) built in ancient times, were demolished... but we still went without shoes for a long time.

In those days you could die even from desperation... and I want to tell you about such bitterness.

One summer afternoon, from the look-out of St. Agostino, my friends and I saw a crowd of people thronging Madonna delle Virtù road: they were all looking into the ravine.

Our curiosity roused, we went down. I was the oldest of us five friends, I was twelve and I understood immediately that something dreadful had happened. An old peasant woman told all those present that she had noticed from far away a woman who climbed onto the fencing wall and let herself fall into the ravine.

"Poor woman!" one of the bystanders said "who knows what was the matter with her!". We were not particularly disturbed by the event: every so often in the Sassi someone died not by natural means, considering the times of extremely straitened circumstances. That same evening I learned from my father that the woman who had thrown herself into the ravine was the mother of one of my friends who were playing with me that afternoon.

INSIDE THE MUSEUM: TANNER'S SHOP

Inside the Museum: peasants' typical house

The bed of manure
(story of F. P., 75 years old)

At three in the morning my father, at the back of the dwelling, the 'lamione', cleaned the floor of the stall, which was paved with large flagstones or 'chianche' that allowed the urine to drain out along the cracks.

Then, with a shovel and a wicker basket, he spread some straw which would facilitate the accumulation of the manure afterwards.

From the platform above the stall where five of us (two girls and three boys) slept, we were invaded by a strong stench that, by a conditioned reflex, we knew heralded the departure for the fields.

Finally, when the cart was positioned with its back to the door and the mules were harnessed, and the pile of manure was loaded, our father prompted us to dress and take our places on the steaming hot layer covered with a canvas sheet.

The whole thing was arranged so that there was a gentle slope which facilitated a more comfortable rest during the journey.

Due to the cold and the discomfort that the job entailed (but you had to do your part to support the family!) that warmth seemed to us more comfortable than the bed of corn husks which we slept on at night.

The "ciddaro"
(story of V.M., 80 years old)

I remember the time when my grandfather took me to a "ciddaro" (a tavern): I can still feel his big hand clasping mine in the smoke-blackened cave and the noise of the men sitting at the tables.

The black cloaks strewn untidily all around seemed to belong to so many ogres gathered there; the hats pulled down over their faces, faces thin and furrowed that showed men from another world; their language, too, was incomprehensible thanks to the confusion of so many different conversations.

There were so many of them: labourers, shepherds, craftsmen. Several were playing cards; some shouted for wine; others were eating bread with anchovies, olives and a piece of cheese; yet others made their way to the door, staggering.

With haunted eyes and silently, they set off for their homes, reflecting that in a few hours' time they would have to set out on their carts, accompanied only by their centuries-old solitude.

INSIDE THE MUSEUM: COPPERSMITH'S SHOP

INSIDE THE MUSEUM: THE CIDDARO

The day of my First Communion
(story of F.A., 79 years old)

"One day a relative of mine" my old aunt told me "left me to look after her baby who was sleeping in a very high cradle.

That was a very big day for me: a few hours previously I had made my First Communion and I was very happy. I had gone to her house, all dressed in white, to receive a gift: in those days it was customary to make the rounds of relations, to share with them the joyful occasion and in return be given some dried figs, biscuits, nuts and so on.

As soon as she saw me the woman asked me to keep an eye on the baby for a few minutes as she had to go out to deal with an important matter. 'If the baby wakes up' she instructed me 'rock him and he'll go to sleep again at once'. Then she went out and I remained there on my own for over an hour. To me it seemed like eternity, since I had nothing to distract me. Gradually I began to fret about being unable to leave and constrained to interrupt my round of relatives, stifling my vanity on such a special day.

Suddenly the baby began to whimper: I started to rock him, gently at first, then more and more forcefully, so much so that the cradle turned over. The baby burst into a torrent of weeping just at the moment when his mother came back in. 'My dear girl' she said in dismay 'we must cast out his fright'.

She wrapped him in a shawl and rushed to a neighbour who lived near Via Muro. I stood stock still in the room, not knowing whether to go away or to wait. I stayed there, dying of fright because I thought I had done something dreadful. The woman returned much later and told me the baby was better; the neighbour had made the sign of the cross repeatedly over the baby's forehead, the baby has yawned again and again, sure sign that the fear was abating; meanwhile she had prayed to St. Anthony and promised him that, if everything went well, she would make her son wear a habit like the saint's for three years. That day, which should have been unforgettable for me was the worst day of my life".

The little king
(story of B. R., 76 years old)

On the grain-chest I played at being king. It was a way to help me to fall asleep and not to think about falling off when I was unconscious: that had happened sometimes but I hadn't cried. The schoolteacher had said that kings never cried.

My father had put a straw-filled mattress on the chest and told me: "Be careful not to fall off!" and blew out the candle.

During the night I could hear the mule kicking near the manger: it made me so cross! The stall was bigger than our one-roomed home but he kicked, he was restless: even the mule had his problems. He was born to die of fatigue, he had no hopes of the pleasures of love: he was castrated to make him work harder.

We were crowded in our house, like sardines in a tin. All living in one room accustomed you to other people's noises, to body odours, to "the creek of the bed-springs", to the afflictions of the constipated, to the moans of grandmother, to the movement of the next-door neighbour who, in the darkness, sounded like ghosts.

"It takes a while to get used to smells" my mother told me "and then you won't notice them anymore!". But I can never forget the stink of urine. We suffered from the smell of the mule and he suffered from ours.

Early in the morning, when the door was thrown open, you could hear hundreds of others doing the same. You couldn't smell the odours any more as in the meantime hunger pangs took precedence.

A light breakfast and then away to school, with sleep in the corner of your eyes and dirty knees.

So many steep ladders to scale in order to become a teacher!

My father, to tell you the truth, would have preferred me to be a farm-hand.

On the grain-chest, at night, before dropping off to sleep, I pretended to be king and thought: "All kings, when they address their subjects, do not say 'I am gone', they know how to work things out and their animals' stalls are not larger than their castles".

INSIDE THE MUSEUM: COBBLER'S SHOP

INSIDE THE MUSEUM: THE GRAIN-CHEST (XVIII CENT.)

The Devil's sweat
(story by N.P, 74 years old)

"The smell is always the same" I was told by a very old visitor "even though it has been restored here.

The sweat of the Devil covered furniture and clothes; gradually wood-worm and moths ate away everything; it oozed out of every pore of our house, even my grandmother said so: it came from far away, from next door, from above, from below, who knows. Drop by drop, slow but relentless, as life flows by.

For us dampness always had been a mystery and children died from it too.

At dawn, when I left for the fields, my trousers and shirt were already cold. Sometimes my wife, when the fire was lit in the kitchen, would put them near the weak flame of olive brambles, so as to lessen my discomfort.

The smell of mould is unique: it has haunted us for years, even when we changed our house in the Sassi. It seemed like a punishment of the Devil...".

Clean up, my girl

Clean up, daughter
the dung that the mule,
in passing,
has left in front of the side-board,
like a streak of blood.
He has a stomach ache, poor animal,
from so much hard work.
Now he will have a rest in the stall
and tomorrow he'll be well again, God willing.

Clean up, my girl
I must prepare the beans in the large dish,
because your father has come back from the fields
and is hungry.
It doesn't matter, my girl:
grandmother is forgiven for everything
when she isn't well,
like the mule
which we are all so fond of.

1954: Visit of Senator E. Colombo to the house in the Sassi of a family aspiring to the assignation of a new housing (ph. Evangelista)

THE MULES (PH. MASCIANDARO)

The broody hen

The hen is hatching under the bed;
husband can't you hear the rustle?
The eggs are opening
in the silence of the room
our hearts fill with joy
we'll have lots of chicks that will grow into hens.

The hen is hatching under the bed.
On the bed children are born
they will work on the land
they will go to war
they will close their eyes in eternal rest
consumed by fever.

My beautiful St. Rita,
let the chicks stay with the hen
let the children grow into men
who will soil their hands with earth
and will not go to war
to kill other mother's sons.

THE WAR

1936: Fascist demonstration in via Fiorentini, Sasso Barisano (ph. Buonsanti)

Hands

There are hands that speak,
that transform the shapeless matter
and know the hard work.
Hands that give joy and pain,
that give a face to the rough stone,
the women's body sinuosity
to an olive stock,
the appearance of the live to the anonymous tufo.

Hands heavy and light as butterflies...
It's the miracle of the hands
which take orders
only from the ancient heart
of the which they know
wisdom and love.

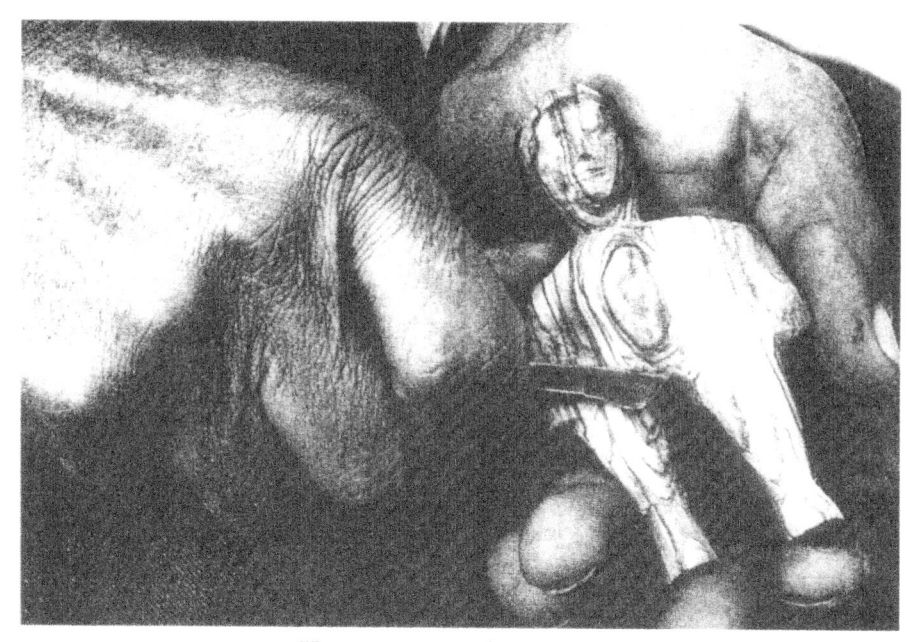

HANDS CARVING (PH. CRESCI)

DE GASPERI IN VIA D'ADDOZIO (1950)

Grandmother's stories
(story of M.R.F., 85 years old)

My grandmother couldn't read nor write but she knew lots of stories that she related to us every evening around the brazier.

We hung on her lips, wide-eyed and all ears; she didn't often repeat any part of the story.

Her face changed according to the course of the story: for the pleasant parts her expression softened and she spoke slowly in her strong dialect; for the unpleasant parts she frowned and she spoke rapidly so as to give more weight to her words and to make her feelings clearer.

Only then would you notice the infinity of wrinkles that lined her old face, once very beautiful.

Her best stories were "The Avaricious Peasant" and "Godmother Death". I remember them well and I want to narrate them to you so that they will not be forgotten.

The avaricious peasant

Once upon a time long ago there was an avaricious peasant who had many carts, mules, arable land, vineyards and money he kept hidden under a stone in his house.

He lived in the Casale area and frequently lent money to the poor farm-hands and artisans who were in difficulties, demanding in payment, instead of monetary interests, their possessions; when one of them was unable to pay back the loan, he took his cart or mule or both; if the debtor was a farm-hand, he took his tools. Anyway, they were possessions that had cost a lot and had meant enormous sacrifices.

The money-lender had no children and that made him very unhappy, especially at night before going to sleep. He said to his wife: "I'm very poor without children" and he turned his back on her with an irritating rustle of dry leaves and pretended to be asleep.

When he was approaching old age and he suffered from insomnia, he said to his wife one day, in a particularly serious tone: "I have no children but I have several nephews and nieces: they are no offspring of mine and I don't want to leave them anything because they hang around me for my money and not for affection".

One afternoon he took all his money out of the hiding-place and went into the country with his cart. Once there he lit a fire, burnt all his money, put the ashes into a jar and filled the jar with water.

That evening, back home, he said: "Wife, I have burnt the cause of all my problems and now they can't upset anyone starting from me!"

Having said that, he started to drink the concoction and drunk it to the last drop, under the eyes of his wife who, recovering from her astonishment, replied: "What idiocy have you committed? If you die now, where shall I find the money for your burial?"

While the man started to writhe in pain from a terrible stomach-ache, his wife concluded in dialect: "They came from water and they go back to water!" with reference to money not earned from honest work.

Godmother Death

A man and a woman were married for many years but their marriage had not been blessed with a child, and, for that reason, believing that the time allotted to them by God was nearly expended, they started to hate each other. Sometimes they teased each other, playfully at first and then spitefully: other times they discussed, without ever reaching a logical conclusion, on the meaning of life and death: why does it happen that one day our life on earth is interrupted and a new life commences?

When they had lost all hope, a miracle happened: a daughter was born. To tell the truth, the woman had, for some months prior to the birth, had a recurring dream: an old woman had told her that, if she was patient, a baby would be born to whom she would be godmother.

The baby was already a few months old when one morning an old woman, very humble, knocked on the door of their house: "I am the godmother of your daughter" she said to the incredulous woman. "Arrange a party, the most important event of your life must be shared with your friends, with great joy and participation."

The husband, less trusting than his wife, thought immediately that this old woman was different from others: she seemed to be too sure of herself, as though she knew something that they could not grasp. Her eyes were cold, composed: she always waited for the other to speak first. The man was convinced that he was confronted by Death, but he didn't lose heart, in fact he asked her to resolve the riddle that he had never understood: the meaning of life and death.

The old woman didn't reply at once, she took his hand and escorted him into a room lit by candles of different lengths and explained: "It's very simple: the candles burn and when they go out that's the end of a life." The man, his heart in his mouth, asked her to show him which candle was his and Death indicated one that was nearly burnt out beside one that was very tall. He understood everything and cried in anguish: "Well then I'm nearing the end! Couldn't I change my candle with the one next to it?" "No" Death replied dryly "In fact go home and I'll join you shortly" she replied with authority.

FAMILY OF AN ARTISAN (1936); A PHOTOMONTAGE WAS MADE TO INCLUDE A SON WHICH WAS SERIOUSLY ILL AT THAT TIME

CHILDREN OF AN ARTISAN IN THE SASSO CAVEOSO (1915)

The laundry
(story of A.M., 83 years old)

When I was a child, between the tasks of emptying the sewage in the town sewer and doing the laundry, I preferred the latter. The worst thing was doing both of them, and sometimes happened.

My mother used to reclaim everyday a little bit of ashes from the economic kitchen and the brazier. Once cold, the ashes were stored in a big basket with a white cloth sewed inside, to avoid the loss of ashes when the basket was moved from one place to another.

The real struggle started with the supplying of water, which was drawn from public fountains in higher rates than usual (to cook, drink and water the animals) for few days. My older sister had the task of carrying the bigger *rizzola* [2], I had to carry the smaller one along the eighty meters between home and the fountain.

Each time we emptied the containers in a big chestnut vat that we used also for the winepress.

When my mother was young things were even more difficult, as public fountains were not installed yet and she had to reach the wells in Piazza Vittorio Veneto to draw rainy water collected in the *Palombaro Lungo*, a huge underground cistern wide as the entire square. Sometime my grandfather asked our neighbours – which had an in-house cistern – to draw some water, not always successfully especially in dry periods.

We did laundry twice a month, but someone did it once for lack of time.

Water was boiled outdoor, when the weather was good...oh yes, we used to do so many things in the *vicinato* [3]: we used to wash wool before spinning and we hang it on poles fixed in the wall to let it dry; we used to wash wide cloths woven with loom for olive harvesting and the wood cases for the vintage; we used to wash vegetables and boil the tomatoes to prepare tomato sauce... The *vicinato* was fundamental for suggestion and advice in uncertain situations... It was also the place for innocent gossip: the virtue of *commara* Maria who died few days before, the sorrow of compare Giuseppe desperate for the death of his mule... In the *vicinato* hopes and illusions *reflourished* and dreams were born...

Anyway, going back to the laundry: in rainy days we used to boil up water near the shed, because its clay ground was good to absorb the liquid that overflowed during the water boiling.

My father used to prepare the fire with cob-cores, dry dung, pine-needles, oak and olive-tree branches, then he put on the fire an iron tripod with a container filled with water upon it. When the water was boiling, it was used to scrub the laundry on a wooden table using a self-made soap, made with pig-fats and soda. Afterwards, we had to prepare the lye to disinfect linen and remove stains. My mother covered with a white rag a big terracotta container and tied it with a rope along the border. Inside the container, the laundry which has been previously scrubbed was placed tidily. Once the cloth was in place upon the container, she put a two fingers-layer of ashes on it and started to pour hot water in. She never forgot to cover the laundry with bay leaves, to have them scented. Once the cloth with ashes was removed, the linen was stirred with wooden sticks for several hours and finally was rinsed out with warm water.

Lye was reclaimed and used for hair-washing, floor and kitchenware cleaning... it was really miraculous!

---

[2] Terracotta container.

[3] Group of houses with entrances overlooking a common area, which was central in the social life of the peasants in the Sassi.

Ten nails and more

One nail to hold the pig,
two to hang garlic and tomatoes,
three to crucify,
four to fix the wooden plough.

He keeps on hitting the red-hot iron,
a long fiery cordon.
Then the little man tightens it
with large pinchers,
and makes so many nails on the anvil,
long and short ones.
One by one
he puts them in the stone tub
and lines them on the iron bench.
He sighs thoughtfully.
Another cordon, in the forge,
ready to be worked.
It seems he wants to crush his anger,
for how he hits and hits again.
The noise is stunning.

Five nails for the kneading trough,
six to hang the clothes on the wall,
seven to affix a smile,
eight to repair the door,
nine to nail his mother's coffin.

The smell of burning coal
comes out from the cave
and mixes with the aroma
of fresh-baked bread.

The killing of the pig
(story of O.F., 89 years old)

Every time the pig had to be killed, for me it was a very sad day. Today there are modern and immediate ways to kill an animal, like a gunshot to its head: the death is instantaneous.

When I was young it was different: I used to hide myself covering my ears to avoid hearing the pig torment. Four or five people were necessary to immobilize it: the animal sensed that it would be death in a while and became capable of enormous strength trying to save itself.

The men stuck a stick into the pig throat and, when its strength began to fail it, they cut its throat at the jugular. The warm blood came out in spurts, and was collected in a bucket: it was used to make sanguinaccio [4], which I liked very much.

In my hidden place, with eyes closed and ears covered, I cannot avoid to remember all the times I played with that pig, when it was baby and my parents before going to work in the fields advised me "keep an eye on the pig because, when the time will come, we will enjoy it... ".

The pig ate anything and grew up day by day; my brothers and I watched at it fancying about eating bread with lard and salami...

The sausages, pieces of lard and the ventresca [5] were hung in the house for the aging: it was really a fragrant and appetizing ornament for our house-cave.

However, we used to sell the better parts of the pork, to buy the things that we needed in the fields or at home...

I can remember as it was today the big pig bleeding tied up to an iron ring and I still have in my ears his heart-breaking howl, that could be heard all over the quarter.

---

[4] Sweet cream made with pig blood, cocoa powder and other spices.
[5] Pork underbelly.

The goat

It was tied two steps from the nanny-goat,
the billy-goat.
The nanny-goat was supine, on the iron table,
the legs tightened up with a rope,
the head reclined,
looking at the billy-goat
for the last time.

Then, a clean cut slit its carotid:
the warm blood flowed
into the bowl underneath.
The very last nanny-goat trembles
weren't caught by anyone,
as for its glazed stare
at the cold iron hook.
The billy-goat was watching all this
without flinching.

"I feel like the sorrow will kill him"
I confided to the expert in charge;
"I don't think so, goats are stupid",
He replied firmly.
"Maybe a little bit less than us",
I thought bitterly.

The lamb
(story of C. F., 85 years old)

Characters: St Peter (SP); Christ (C); the Death (D); a greengrocer (G)

St Peter, Christ and the Death met one day and decided to roast a lamb to celebrate. The Saint knew a greengrocer which owned some sheep and came to him, to buy a lamb.
SP: – Greengrocer, I would need a lamb.
G: – Who are you to ask me this?
SP: – I'm St Peter, the founder of Catholic Church.
G: – I'm sorry, there's nothing for you here because of your partiality; in fact with your keys you open Heaven gates just for some souls, sending the others to Hell.
The saint came away unhappy and told Christ and the Death what happened. "I'm sure he won't deny me the lamb" Christ said and started for greengrocer's house.
"Who's knocking?" asked the greengrocer coughing.
"I'm Christ, and I come to buy the lamb that you refused to give to St. Peter". "The answer is still negative, – the man replied – as you promise the Heaven to everybody, even those who don't deserve it". So, Christ came away disappointed in the house where the others were.
"I'm sure he won't deny me the lamb", the Death stated.
"Who's knocking?" asked the greengrocer coughing.
"I am the Death and I come to ask for the lamb which you know".
"For you there is everything you want, as you made no distinction among men: in front of you they are actually all equal".

1891: FAMILY OF AN ARTISAN (AUTHOR'S ANCESTORS)

Il mistero della SEMPLICITÀ

"...IN THE MUSEUMS THERE ARE MEN'S FACES TO TELL A STORY."

Hands, voices and faces for a Museum

In the churches there's place for Saints,
in the museums there are men's faces
to tell a story.

A thousand unknown hands
built up these tools,
a thousand unknown voices
wove their affairs.
Still they are all in museums: hands, voices and faces,
to make us think.
How much strength give the sorrow?
A people need much of it to grow up.

Rasola

With long, bony hands,
with blue veins in relief
my grandma makes
thinner a stripe of pasta.
She prepared it before,
with so much love,
on a spruce board.

With the corner of the *rasola* [6]
she cut the *orecchietta* [7]
and she worked it with forefinger and thumb.
They are all equal and golden:
she put them in columns as soldiers,
looking at them with sweetness.

Today her sharpness is softened.
Once in a while she casts sidelong glances at me,
like I was an intruder.

---

[6] Tool to make hand-made pasta
[7] Shape of pasta

Proofs of bravery

You stay by the door of your home
to watch the star in the sky
which saw your birth.
With Sunday shoes
you walk slowly
to enjoy the way
which you walked many times
whitened with lime
and dripping with sweat,
bent for tiredness.

That is not your home any more.

Now the sleep is shorter and shorter,
and memories lays up,
fermenting like must,
in the long summer wakings…

Those huge slices of stale bread,
wet and sugared,
with a little bit of cheese
or a little slice of third-class *mortadella* [8];
or just bread with smell of something,
sat on a stone, among the others,
with bare feet and snotty noses.
Quick as lizards and thin
as bunches of dry bushes …

Those races downhill, with no escape,
three upon a board on ball-bearings,

collected begging for them everywhere.
The first proofs of bravery:
how many after those!
You have lost count.

---

[8] Bologna sausage.

Prayers and spells

In Lucania magic and religion were mixed up, favouring the maintaining of a disputable social equilibrium: the poor felt comforted by promises about afterlife and not responsible for their own destiny of which they weren't masters; consequently the rich could easily preserve their privileges and predominant position, consolidated along centuries.

The Church was indulgent with superstition and magic practices: the abolition of those would have meant the risk that people developed the consciousness of the need to act to determine their own life, depending only on the choices and the willing of each person.

The consciousness of the rights, for which would have been worth to fight, could possibly determine social and politic upsets which would have been problematical for riches and clergy that had goods and privileges.

The main theme of magical practices was the fascination, that is the transmission of a power to someone to limit his autonomy and determine specific behaviours.

To perform a common fascination, the witch dissolved nine pinches of salt and put out three burning embers in a container full of water: with the coal signed the forehead of the patient and then said one Our father, one Hail Mary and one Glory Be.

To captivate a woman, a man had to put in his mattress a little woollen plait, sign of union; according to Cabbala recommendations, was advisable to act in uneven months.

To fascinate a man, women used menstrual blood, pubic hair or particular love potions: the woman pricked her right little finger to get three drops of blood that were mixed with pubic hairs and dried in the oven for the bread; the potion was taken to church during Mass celebration; at the time of Elevation, the magical spell had to be pronounced.

The complexity of the rituals was almost a guarantee of effectiveness.

Many girls, to have available menstrual blood when needed, used to store it in a little bottle and "consecrated" it with this spell: "blood of my nature, preserve until my burial".

It also existed "black" fascination: in many towns of Lucania, wedding processions followed exactly the same way to church and back home, and they jumped across church entry being afraid to fall over the *legamento*, a little rope with many knots made by a possible rival in love, prepared following a specific ritual with spells mixed with prayers. For the same reason, not just as symbol of man's domination on the woman, the bridegroom crossed their home entry carrying the bride in his arms.

During the marriage, if a candle blew out from the bride side it was considered a negative foreboding.

There were also several remedies to cancel the effects of those practices: at the four corners of the double sheet, grains of wheat, salt pinches and pins were placed; scissors and scythes were put under the mattress, a piece of the rope from church bell was placed under the bed, a broom was placed near the house entry (reference to witches) to keep out negative power.

Many rituals were used to test lover's fidelity: a lit candle was taken near an open window, if it blew out, there was infidelity, otherwise the fidelity was certain.

They also trusted to sounds: dog barking meant loyalty, water downpour was negative sign, hearing footsteps meant that the lover was going to come back.

As conclusion of any ritual or spell, prayers had to be said, as guarantee of the authenticity of the response.

The little peasant

It was a long time ago since the obsession to collect ethnographic objects was a fever that burnt in my heart.

It was tiring but at the same time I enjoyed it.

I emptied basements, attics and sheds.

The yellowed photos of men aged for hard work, with anonymous thin faces, collected in the most strange places, are strong testimonies of a not-so-far past, spread along the Museum path.

The little peasant recognized in one of those photos by a distant relative emigrated to Canada, who visited the Museum, now has his own history.

In 1968 he decided to seek fortune elsewhere with his wife and seven children, running away from a cold new housing received in change of an animal shelter in the Sasso Barisano.

I saw the serene, ninety-years-old little peasant wife on the internet, with my book in her hands opened at the page where she and her husband, thin and serious, were been immortalized in the most important day of their lives, away back in 1940.

She enjoys good health, like she had never been in the circle of Hell of the Sassi. Even from so far away she contributed as well in writing our memory and I'm grateful to her for this. I look at the little peasant on page 55 with pride: I feel like I had known him all my life.

PORTRAIT OF THE AUTHOR BY JOACHIM KLINGER

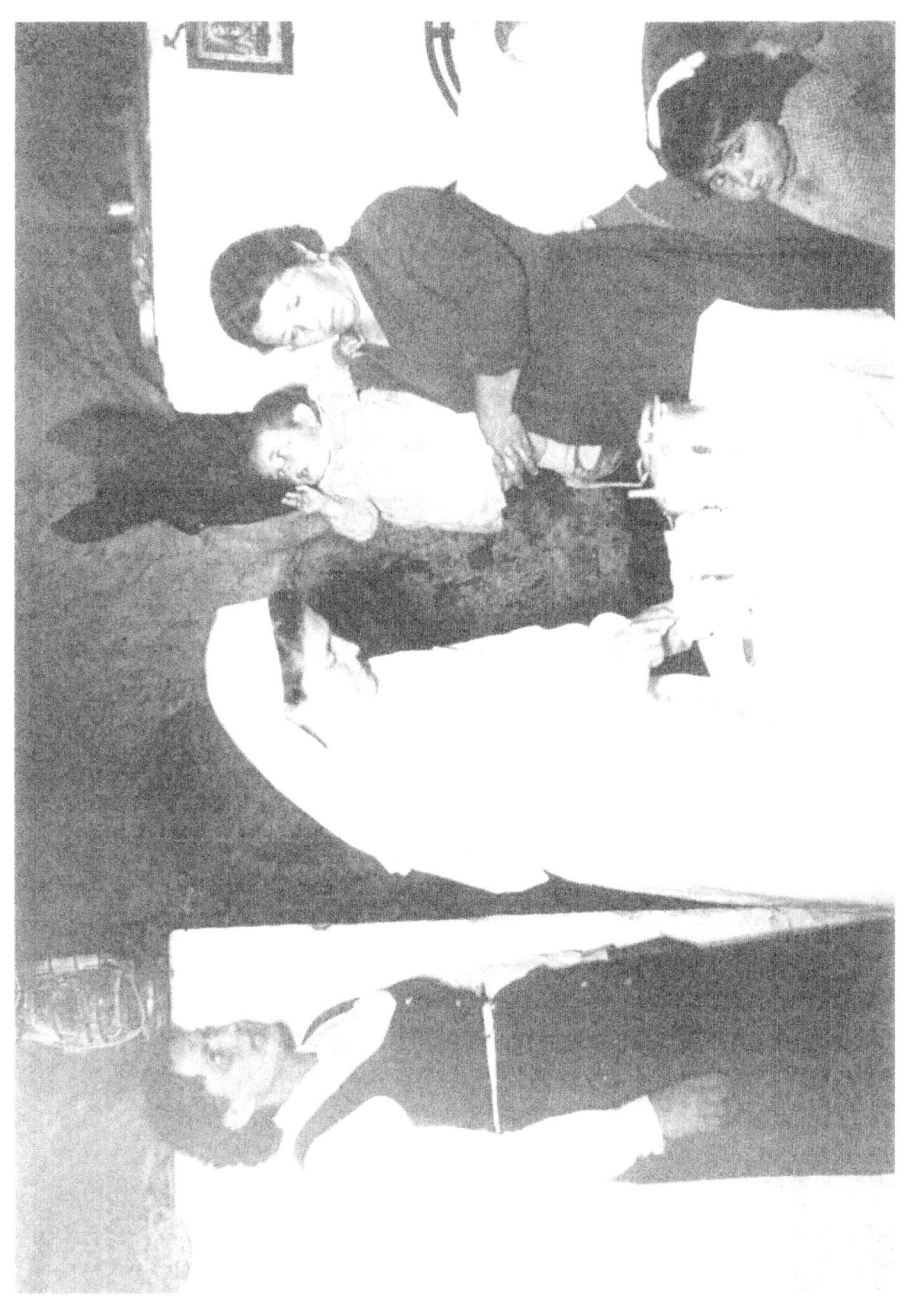

"When the Museum was inhabited...". Compulsory vaccination at home, during the Fascism

The vaccination
(story of M.C., 89 years old)

The old woman was very touched while she was handing me the photo.

"The day before they came, I cleaned up all the house: a cave with few things, a cistern near the bed, a white wall with the height of a man to separate people from the mule.

The animal couldn't take its sad eyes off us in the day of the vaccination: sometimes they seemed to implore, sometimes to wait, when it had to stay at home because my husband had something else urgent to do and couldn't go to the field.

In the days before, with the neighbours, I talked a lot about these new medicines which should have protected our children from a lot of diseases and, consequently, I was waiting anxiously for the arrival of the nurse.

I can remember perfectly, as it was today...

At that time I was thirty and I had four children: two twin seven years old daughters, and two sons seven years and six months old.

I washed the children with care in a zinc tub, using well water heated on the fireplace, then I dressed them with the poor dresses they used every day.

I put a white accurately ironed tablecloth, the same I used to rise the dough for the bread, on the table to be used to set down medicines and syringes.

That day, to make a good impression, I wore the earrings my husband gave me for our engagement; the dress, however, was the same I wore every day.

I made my daughters wear small silver earrings as well, which I received from a merchant exchanging it with my cut plaits.

When the nurse and the social worker finally came, I wanted the ground to swallow me up. The girl was very well-groomed: she wore a white blouse under a brown pinafore with an thin elegant belt.

Instead the nurse looked strict and her white gown made me feel very uneasy.

The social worker made me a lot of questions: if I wanted to leave the cave, if I attended school, the number of my children... While she was speaking to me, she wasn't looking at me; she was looking at the walls of the cave. Now and then her eyes met mine and I looked down, ashamed and uneasy.

Her detachment hurt me: I felt, behind her apparent understanding, she hid a deep contempt, I don't know either for us or the institutions she represented.

The nurse quietly carried out her job, joked with the twins and gave them some candies; she recommended to look for her at the hospital in case of need.

Then, they quickly made their way toward other houses, where poor women like me were waiting".

It was the time

It was the time when the poor walked pigs and turkeys outdoor – as for the dogs today – using a leash made of several pieces of rope or obtained using twisted rags, since they didn't had any other space for their animals but the *lamione* [9] or the house-cave where they used to live as well.

It was the time when burning braziers were placed outside until charcoal turned into embers; the braziers were then brought inside, after having made the sign of the cross.

It was the time when the woman used to wait for her man by the door, with his cart full of implements and, perhaps, of food.

It was the time when new people were succeeding the former, forging characters, languages and architectures: there was much poverty and the willing, sometimes, faded away.

It was the time to reach illusory achievements, to conclude what we define today as "Peasant Culture".

---

[9] Built house that extended a pre-existing cave.

The little twin girls

– Let's go to that house,
I can hear wails! –
We run, scrambling breathlessly
across wagons and mules.
I remember a game
that was not a game.
We are finally inside:
one room; at bottom,
the bad-smelling barn.
The flies, the half-light,
the torments, the pale faces
of men and women;
the silent mule
stares at us, as if it blamed us
for the indiscretion of being there.
Everyone is around two dumplings
of flesh wrapped in white bandages,
on a high bed; their little brothers,
some barefoot and some not,
have adult gaze in their eyes.

In one moment we are already outside,
wrapped in heat and fear.
Since that day I have grown up
quickly.

The miracle of tears

It wasn't enough crossing
yourself and the bread
to be protected from the fear.
It could be heard in the night
rubbing one stone on another:
it wasn't the mule kicking,
nor the craftsman beating.
There was no moon, no stars:
nothing that could alleviate
your pains.
You had tougher hands
than those of a man:
they knew how to caress the grain
under the sun that stole
what was left of your smile.
And you kneaded,
you worked the "treasure",
with firm and ancient gestures;
you wrapped it lovingly,
like a child in a woolen rag,
and you made it warm
under the covers "of the soul of God".
The miracle was rising
slowly:
from tears only arose
a flower that lasted one day.

The people's feast

Crowded as ever:
today is the feast of saints and believers.
An impressive echo is heard from afar,
it is a riot of lights and watercolors.
The *madonnari* draw Madonnas on the pavement
with the faces of common women, rosy and self-confident,
which will only last a few hours.
Flashes of light leap from one coin
to another and the artist observes in silence:
he may be counting or thinking to another feast.
Then priests, policemen, horses and riders.
Thousands of shoes dragging
on colored chalks.
Angels, cherubs, doves, columns and crosses
are wobbling on the Chariot
for the last race: a thousand colors
are melting and shattering
in the tearing of paper and cardboard.
Eyes laughing and crying.
Mouths screaming and getting angry.
Someone, with arms up, is holding
the hard-earned artifacts.
The wonderful anxiety of the people subsides
when the Chariot is torn apart as well as the devil.
Finally, like endless rows of processionaries,
they reach the fireworks; the night is long
and lights up as in daylight. A thousand falling stars,
dreamy flowers that burn; everyone expresses
a desire while thinking to the next
even more beautiful feast.

The ring
(story of F.D., 94 years old)

"The day the fascist government decided everyone must contribute with gold, copper and iron to the growth of Italy, it was my tenth birthday.

My parents took the news badly.

– They give with one hand and take with the other! – said my father, referring to the cash prizes they gave to large families. Ours was a life of hardship, like that of so many others, and of narrow hopes. It was not uncommon that a few months old child died, and the prize was postponed to another birth.

Specific procedures were established for the collection of gold and metals. Every beginning of the week, a person in charge with some helpers went around the families and checked if there were more than three copper or aluminum pots in the house; the surplus was piled up in a pickup truck. Gates, railings, disused plows and ferrous materials of various kinds were collected as well.

Same thing was to happen to wedding rings, pendants, brooches and everything was made with gold; for those precious items, however, a specific collection day was defined for the whole national territory. To certify the delivery, of course, a receipt with proper stamp and fascist secretary signature was released.

– They came the 18th of December 1935, the day when all Italians were called to donate their gold to the homeland.

There was so much sadness that day. At first they took several pots, including the ones in aluminum we used in the countryside for the harvesting of tomatoes; then they continued with the wedding rings, that were exchanged with iron rings with the engraved inscription "Oro alla Patria–18 NOV XIV" [10].

---

[10] *Gold to homeland 18th November 1935.*

My mother's eyes glistened when she saw my father removing from the ring finger his wedding ring to deliver to the officer, with his head low. At the same time, she quickly took off two tiny earrings from her earlobes and said: – This is my little advance for the homeland: my wedding ring fell in the well as it was fitting a little bit loose –. She spoke with so much confidence that all of us believed her immediately; the secretary not too much instead: he looked at her with suspicion and stated that he would have given the order to empty the well as soon as possible.

My mother wasn't impressed at all, and she assured with dignity that during the usual summer cleaning of the well, she would have found the ring for sure.

But in August the well was not cleaned.

The secretary, who didn't forget at all, got very angry and considered my mother's attitude as an offense to the homeland liable to punishment. She didn't lose heart and she tried very calmly to remedy that tense situation.

Among my grandfather's stuff, lost in the First World War, there was a small ring of little value hidden in a patched sock: she took it and let it fall into the official's hand saying: – Now I have no more debt, if debt must be called –.

The secretary, redder than a pepper, nervously closed the front door behind him. We have been a little scared that day, but since then no one came asking for the wedding ring anymore.

The ring was no longer spoken of even in the years following the assignment of the new housing in *Serra Venerdì*, which marked the end of a nightmare and anticipated a widespread and even deeper malaise.

My father died of tuberculosis when he was sixty, when my mother was fifty-four, I was twenty-seven, my brother twenty-nine, my sisters twenty and twenty-four.

In the new neighborhoods the evenings passed in sadness, the streets were not well lit and there were still some open construction sites that spread a sense of disorder and incompleteness.

The people, although happy to have abandoned the unhealthy and decrepit houses in the Sassi, were disoriented and someone, meeting you, did not even say hello not for lack of courtesy, but as if they were afraid of bringing out in a possible conversation the fear that their dream of redemption was beginning to deflate like a balloon.

In 1966, thirteen years after moving to our new home, we left the city and that house that had made us feel good at first and so badly after, since poverty had returned even in the absence of chickens, mules and pigs.

There was no other solution than to change our job and add the American language to our dialect.

Aunt Maria, who left two years before us and was already able to express herself a little in English, made herself available to host us and guide us in our new life.

My mother died when she was ninety. When we dressed her for the burial in the cemetery of Toronto, her wedding ring came out of her pillowcase and began bouncing on the gray floor, reflecting a soft golden light.

We were all stunned and remembered that episode from the past: she had kept that secret for so many years, without even talking about it with her sons and daughters!"

Thank you Francesco for donating your mother's wedding ring, in agreement with your brothers and sisters, to this museum.

It is here, in a showcase, suspended with a ribbon over other jewels of that time.
It gives off an almost human haughtiness and still reflects a warm golden light.

THE WEDDING RING OF FRANCESCO'S MOTHER

A monument to the mule
Afterword by Giovanni Caserta

Fifty years have gone by since Tullio Tentori, a member of the Friedmann study group between 1951 and 1955, carried out his survey on the conditions of the inhabitants of the Sassi. He devised a questionnaire to which the concerned had to answer in writing. The answers were all full of desperation and heartbreak with regards to the possibility of finding work, the sanitary conditions, the most common illnesses, the infant mortality rate, hunger, thirst and discomfort of all sorts. It was even said that not even animals lived in those conditions. The MP Bianco stated in the parliamentary session of 27th February 1951 that "when speaking of the Sassi of Matera, one needs to imagine hell-pits, only ten times worse. One needs to think of dwellings that are the same as those of 5.000 years ago, of dens that the troglodytes of 5.000 years ago clawed out with their fingernails from the rock, one after another, towards the centre of the Earth; one needs to think of dwellings where the sun never enters, nor air nor light, where there is no flooring, and the walls and roof are of living rock, where in short there is nothing human, and where, in 2.997 warrens of less than 3.500 rooms in total, a population of 16.000 inhabitants live; and with them mules, donkeys, pigs and chickens!". People slept where and how they could – as is recalled by Giuseppe L., 84 years old, in this book – "one on a bench, others on the mezzanine, some in the big bed and even someone in a drawer".

Next came the laws on the so-called "reclamation" of the Sassi. Almost all of the inhabitants of the two Sassi quarters were allocated purpose-built housing in the neighbourhoods of Serra Venerdi, Lanera, Spine Bianche, Villa Longo, San Giacomo, Platani, Serra Rifusa, Agna, Pini and La Martella. Many of them, however, had to move from those houses yet again, this time as emigrants, headed for Switzerland, Germany and north Italy. In the meantime, the entrances to the cave dwellings in the Sassi were walled up to avoid squatters taking over; but care was taken in leaving an open gap on the top so that air would circulate. The caves, in fact, as a result of humidity, run a high risk of collapsing during the transition from winter to summer when the tufo, heavy and bloated with dampness, would be prone to crumble while drying up. Then, for over forty years, there was a great deal of talk about the fate of these two quarters of the Sassi.

The whole debate shifted, as expected, onto finding a development solution to the problem. In other words, it was a matter of choosing between destroying and recovering the site. These were difficult options to put into effect. Once destruction was excluded, for practical as well as cultural reasons, there was no other solution left but housing reclamation, itself extremely complex and unprecedented as it involved making an absurd environment, predominantly consisting in caves, fit for habitation. Those advocating the reclamation, mainly architects and planners, as can be easily appreciated, in promoting their argument almost always had to hide the appalling truth of those quarters, that is to say the sub-human conditions of those who had lived there. As a result, an overly aesthetic vision or portrayal of those two settlements prevailed, which almost came to be described as two masterpieces of the human, or of the "peasant" genius. Someone, even, proudly protested against the presumed uncouthness and insensitivity of who, for mere political and electoral interests, had defined the Sassi a "national shame". The allusion was to a memorable speech given by Togliatti in Matera, on 1st April 1948.

All this obviously risked becoming a dangerous mystification of history and reality, even more so because, as the reclamation works were gradually carried out, an inevitable "embellishment" of the two quarters and of the single houses occurred, which were rightly fitted with air conditioning, dehumidifiers and various unifications of buildings, thus leading to the loss of the real nature and image of what those dwellings had been through the centuries. Moreover, the housing reclamation involved only the so-called "palazziate" or built houses; the caves, on the other hand, became cellars, store-rooms or, at best, a room where to spend an evening among friends.

Cascione, with his poet's and artist's soul, and therefore more sensitive than architects and town planners towards people's conditions, foresaw the danger of the loss of memory not so much of the tufo blocks and the rocks, which matter less, but of the people who lived there among privations equal only to what, even today, is seen on television documentaries about the underdeveloped countries. He set about collecting artefacts and documents concerning the "peasant condition", an expression which is perhaps more appropriate than the equivocal and misleading one of "peasant culture". Thus his museum was born. One can say that, as elsewhere sites where torture and other tragic realities had occurred were preserved to avoid "forgetting", so Cascione has gathered together tools and various implements, in other words objects and "signs" which would evoke particular living conditions. Then, over the years, tourists arrived in the museum but also previous inhabitants of the Sassi, all weighed down by the years. Not a few came from the north of Italy and from abroad. Some of them remembered and wrote to him.

It is surprising, but not that much, how all of them offer a recollection of that world that is not in the least idyllic. The only exceptions are a few nostalgic memories of the spirit of solidarity that could be found in the neighbourhood which, if we look at it more carefully – as it has been described on other occasions, and by Tentori himself – was nothing more than a system of "mutual aid", i.e. the result of a primordial necessity of survival and adaptation in periods and places of great poverty and hardship, where the State and the public institutions were altogether absent apart from, only in more recent years and in exceptional cases, the intervention of some bishop and religious order. The fact remains that those visitors, who used to inhabit the Sassi, confirm again what had been stated by those interviewed by Tentori. This means that, fifty years later, their memories have not faded in the least. There is one who experienced and recalls his life as a shepherd boy in the farms, where there used to be in force the strict and unquestionable law of the master and of the headman, who would not think twice about using violence on the youngsters, expecting gratitude from their victims and their parents. It was for their own good – they used to say – as they had to be taught some manners first and a trade after. The same law, albeit partially restrained, was in force in the craftsmen workshops, even towards their own sons. Antonio F., 73 years old and the son of a *carradore* or cart builder, recalls how one day his father, in a fit of temper, threw a spanner at him. He had arrived late at work to help him. He still has the scar on his forehead.

There are those who recall the horrifying sanitary conditions of the cave-dwellings. They used to live with their animals, in the stench of excrements, even human. They used to urinate directly in the stable; for other needs, they used to share a clay pot called *cantero*. Instead of toilet paper there was a rag, variously blotched. In the dark it could happen that one put his hand in others' dirt. And there were those who, to economize, would wash the rag to use it again. It would also happen that the clay pot would fill up before expected. One would then end up sitting, if not sinking, in the filth of an entire family and of any additional guests. The clay pot used to be emptied early in the morning. "Like a thief – recalls Immacolata S., 73 years old – dressed in those few rags that I had, I used to creep through the streets of the Sassi clutching the chamber-pot (in spite of the wooden lid the smell would make me retch). The worst part was cleaning out the pot with the little water available".

In those conditions, illnesses were widespread, unexceptional even. Against them the orthodox medicine was not employed, as it was too expensive. Sorceresses and formulas, halfway between witchery and religion, were used instead. Or they resorted to very dubious empirical remedies. One interviewed by Tullio Tentori stated: "I have three children and each of them has suffered from an illness that can be ascribed to the unhealthy conditions in which we lived, such as malaria, smallpox, conjunctivitis, diphtheria, typhus and paratyphoid fever b". Fifty years later, a visitor of the museum remembers a mouse on the chest of drawers, which would feed every night on the oil of the lamp. Another visitor recalls how easy it was to die. "One winter's evening – he tells – my father brought home Giuseppe huddled up on the saddle of the mule and wrapped in a woollen blanket". It was the 1930s. It had happened that the boy, while in the fields, had felt ill with shivers from fever. He had leant on the cart wheel and had died. In this way several children and young people passed away: like "sparks" they used to say. And neither was it possible to mourn the dead ones for long. Already the day after the burial of Giuseppe the father had gone back to the fields, together with his mule, a constant presence and regular witness of the life in that "inferno", such in the real sense of the word. "There was a time when man and mule – Cascione tells – were one / one flesh / one breath / one single human adventure [...] Nearly brushing it, the mule would pass by the table /

where the woman had set / an enormous dish of *maccheroni* with oil and garlic / Eagerly eyed by the numerous family who waited in silence / watching as the ancient ritual was carried out". The old people, in the new homes assigned to them – Eustacchio P., 80 years, recalls – "couldn't sleep because they missed the breath of the mule on their necks which had been like a lullaby for them, the lullaby that their mothers had deprived them of". Maybe it is worth remembering that the town planners, when they came to planning the houses in La Martella, thought of ensuring to the recipient the possibility of looking at and checking, even during the night, through a little window, the stable and the mule, of which they could hear the "breathing".

Once, while talking of the blacksmith and the art of shoeing the animals in Matera, we suggested that an artist should be commissioned, once and for all, to make a monument to the mule, symbol and synthesis of the economy and the peasant life of Matera, like we can admire today the monument to the labourer and the tinker, or elsewhere, the monument to Pinocchio or to the eagle or to the mountain goat. The mule has always inspired great fondness. It was a hybrid, being the result of a cross between a mare and a donkey. It therefore was sterile and, so, it was destined to never enjoy the pleasures of love. It was customary to neuter it when a foal because, if left "intact", its sexual appetites would become insatiable, furious and dangerous. When neutered, instead, it became meek and docile, yet equally firm and strong in pulling the plough through the clayey earth, the cart along the sloping tracks, fast and lean in carrying the pack-saddle, and on it even two or three people. In other words it was the "vehicle" par excellence, more important than an old man or a child. It is not surprising, then, that on occasion of an illness and his death, people visited to give their condolences.

A monument to this animal could be placed in Via Madonna delle Virtù, in the forecourt where "Porta Pistola" used to be, between the Gravina and the direct access to the Sassi. It was customary, even up the 50s, to "park" there hundreds of carts. In the evenings, especially during the summer, from those carts could be heard the whispers of the young lovers, who had managed to escape the vigilant and watchful surveillance of parents and relatives to go – it was said in the peasant dialect of those days – *trebbiare*, i.e. threshing. Some, under a cart, even organised their elopement.

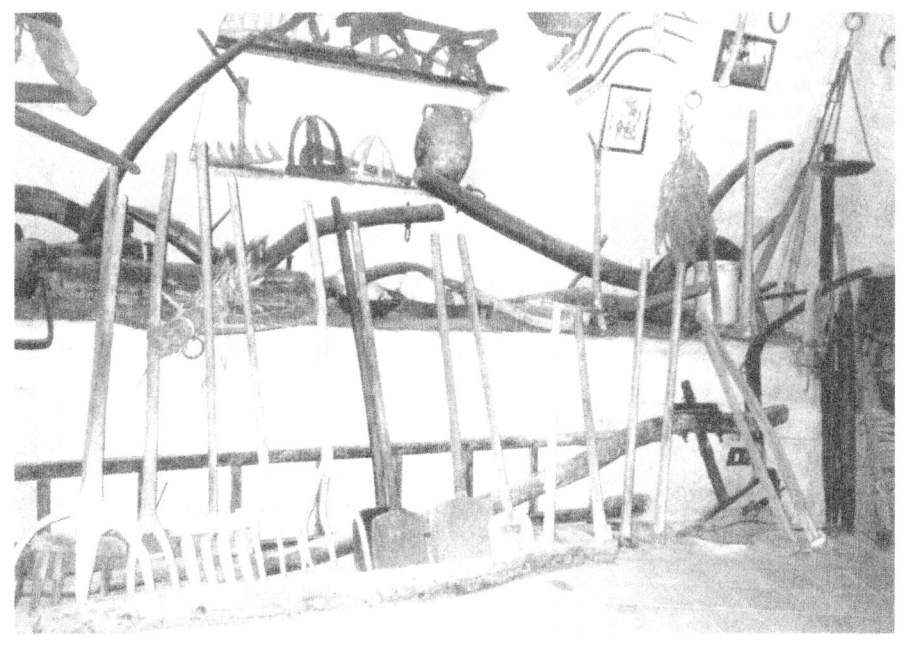

INSIDE THE MUSEUM: AGRICULTURAL TOOLS

Feast of the Madonna della Bruna (1938)

LETTER FOUND IN AN OLD 1930S CHEST

Table of contents (general)

Foreword 1
Objects, memories and tales 5
Author's note 7
Author's note to the second edition 10
Author's notes to the third edition 11
Testimonies of the Museo Laboratorio della Civiltà Contadina
visitors: tales and poems 14
A monument to the mule 132

Table of contents (tales and poems)

Author's notes to the third edition 11
The reasons for this Museum 14
The shepherd boy 15
The brazier 19
The wailing of tiredness 20
Pucc d suunn 20
When even the calls of nature meant hard work 24
The cart builder 25
The donkey 27
U cidd 27
The grain chest 28
Giuseppe 31
The death of children 33
The dead at home 36
The cavapozzi (The well digger) 38
The seamstresses 39
The mouse 43
The cavamonti (The rock digger) 45
Filomena 48
Once defeated, now triumphant 54
The man and the mule 57
A letter from Milan 58
Spindle spindle 62
The new quarters 63
The greys of my houses 68

The glass bell	69
The fountain of love	73
Those men	74
Harvest time	77
The tragedy	78
The bed of manure	81
The "ciddaro"	82
The day of my First Communion	85
The little king	86
The Devil's sweat	90
Clean up, my girl	91
The broody hen	94
Hands	97
Grandmother's stories	100
The avaricious peasant	100
Godmother Death	101
The laundry	105
Ten nails and more	107
The killing of the pig	108
The goat	109
The lamb	110
Hands, voices and faces for a Museum	113
Rasola	114
Proofs of bravery	115
Prayers and spells	117
The little peasant	119
The vaccination	122
It was the time	124
The little twin girls	125
The miracle of tears	126
The people's feast	127
The ring	128

Donato Cascione

Matera, 1949 – Lives and works in Matera

Poetry

L'ultimo pianto (1969)
Sangue e terra magra (1971)
Un altro giorno (1975)
Nel segno del potere la traccia di noi deboli (1977)
Il gioco del tempo (1978)
Accordi in idiosincrasia (1980)
La toppa del sogno (1993)
Il secchio nel pozzo (2015)
I giorni che verranno (2019)

Fiction

Avviso ai naviganti (1980)
Dalla prua scrutando il mare (1990)
Le ossessioni del marinaio (2003)
I racconti del museo (2005)

All Families

Adoptive Families

by C.M. Davis

FOCUS READERS
BEACON

www.focusreaders.com

Copyright © 2023 by Focus Readers®, Lake Elmo, MN 55042. All rights reserved. No part of this book may be reproduced or utilized in any form or by any means without written permission from the publisher.

Focus Readers is distributed by North Star Editions:
sales@northstareditions.com | 888-417-0195

Produced for Focus Readers by Red Line Editorial.

Photographs ©: Shutterstock Images, cover, 1, 4, 11, 20–21, 22; iStockphoto, 7, 8, 13, 14, 17, 19, 25, 27, 29

Library of Congress Cataloging-in-Publication Data
Names: Davis, C. M., author.
Title: Adoptive families / C.M. Davis.
Description: Lake Elmo, MN : Focus Readers, [2023] | Series: All families | Includes index. | Audience: Grades 2-3
Identifiers: LCCN 2022034512 (print) | LCCN 2022034513 (ebook) | ISBN 9781637394564 (hardcover) | ISBN 9781637394939 (paperback) | ISBN 9781637395653 (pdf) | ISBN 9781637395301 (ebook)
Subjects: LCSH: Adoption--Juvenile literature. | Adoptive parents--Juvenile literature. | Adopted children--Juvenile literature. | Interracial adoption--Juvenile literature. | Families--Juvenile literature.
Classification: LCC HV875 .D3528 2023 (print) | LCC HV875 (ebook) | DDC 306.874--dc23/eng/20220721
LC record available at https://lccn.loc.gov/2022034512
LC ebook record available at https://lccn.loc.gov/2022034513

Printed in the United States of America
Mankato, MN
012023

About the Author

C.M. Davis is a librarian and educator. When she's not reading or writing, she enjoys bird-watching, visiting museums, and hunting for vintage treasures in thrift stores.

Table of Contents

CHAPTER 1
Adoption Day 5

CHAPTER 2
Many Ways to Make a Family 9

CHAPTER 3
Questions and Challenges 15

MANY IDENTITIES
All in One 20

CHAPTER 4
Belonging 23

Focus on Adoptive Families • 28
Glossary • 30
To Learn More • 31
Index • 32

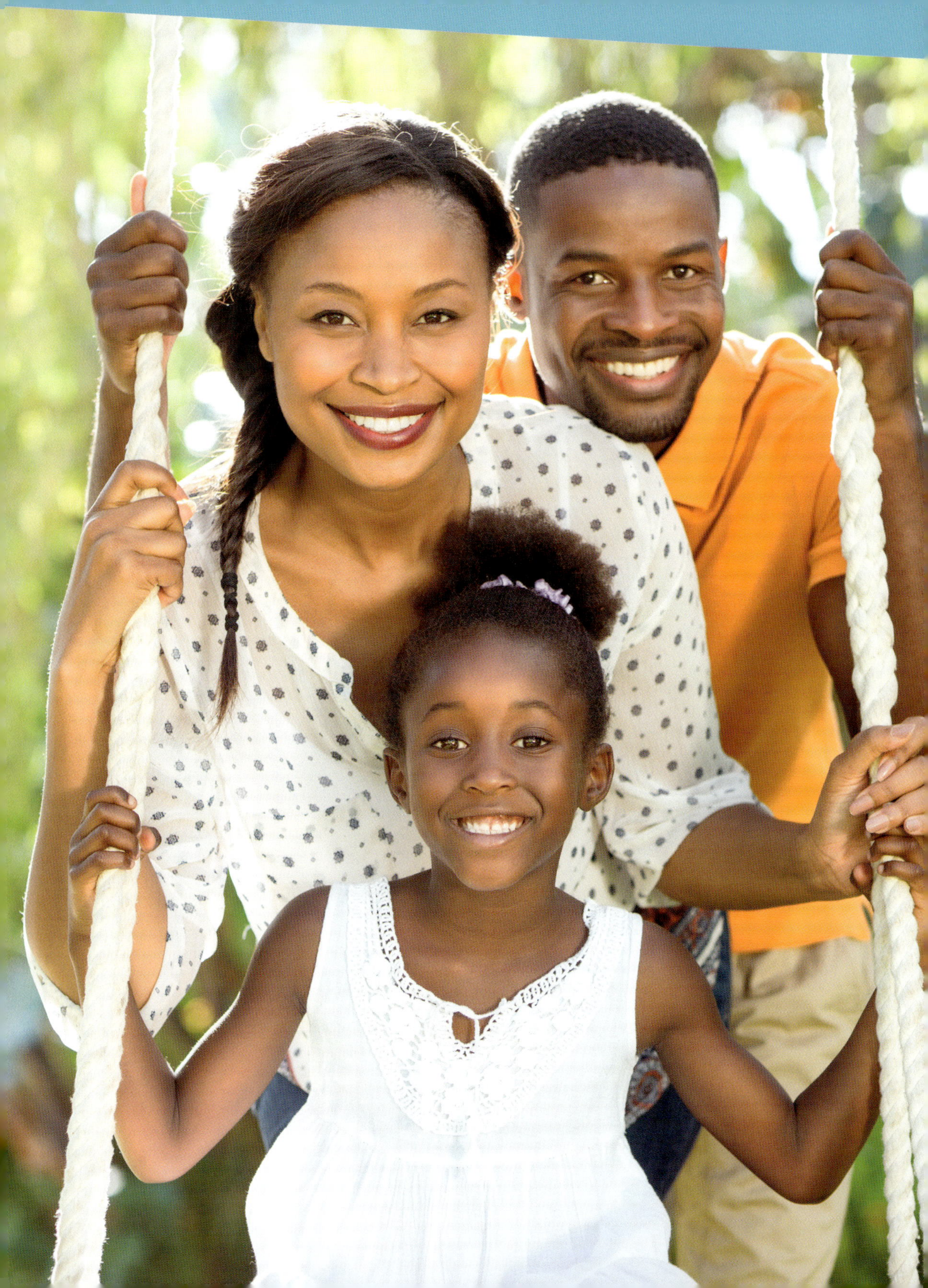

Chapter 1

Adoption Day

A family is celebrating the adoption day of their child. On that day, the parents went to **adoption court**. They stood before a judge. They promised to love and take care of their child.

> Approximately 1 out of 50 US children is adopted.

Then, the parents and child became a family.

The family made plans for the day. First, they played together at a beautiful park. Later, they made tacos for dinner. And for dessert, they had chocolate cupcakes.

Before bedtime, the family read a story. They looked at pictures in

Did You Know?

Adoptive families have been part of human life for thousands of years.

> **Lifebooks can help adopted children answer questions about their past.**

the child's lifebook. A lifebook tells a child about their birth family. It also tells a child about their adoptive family.

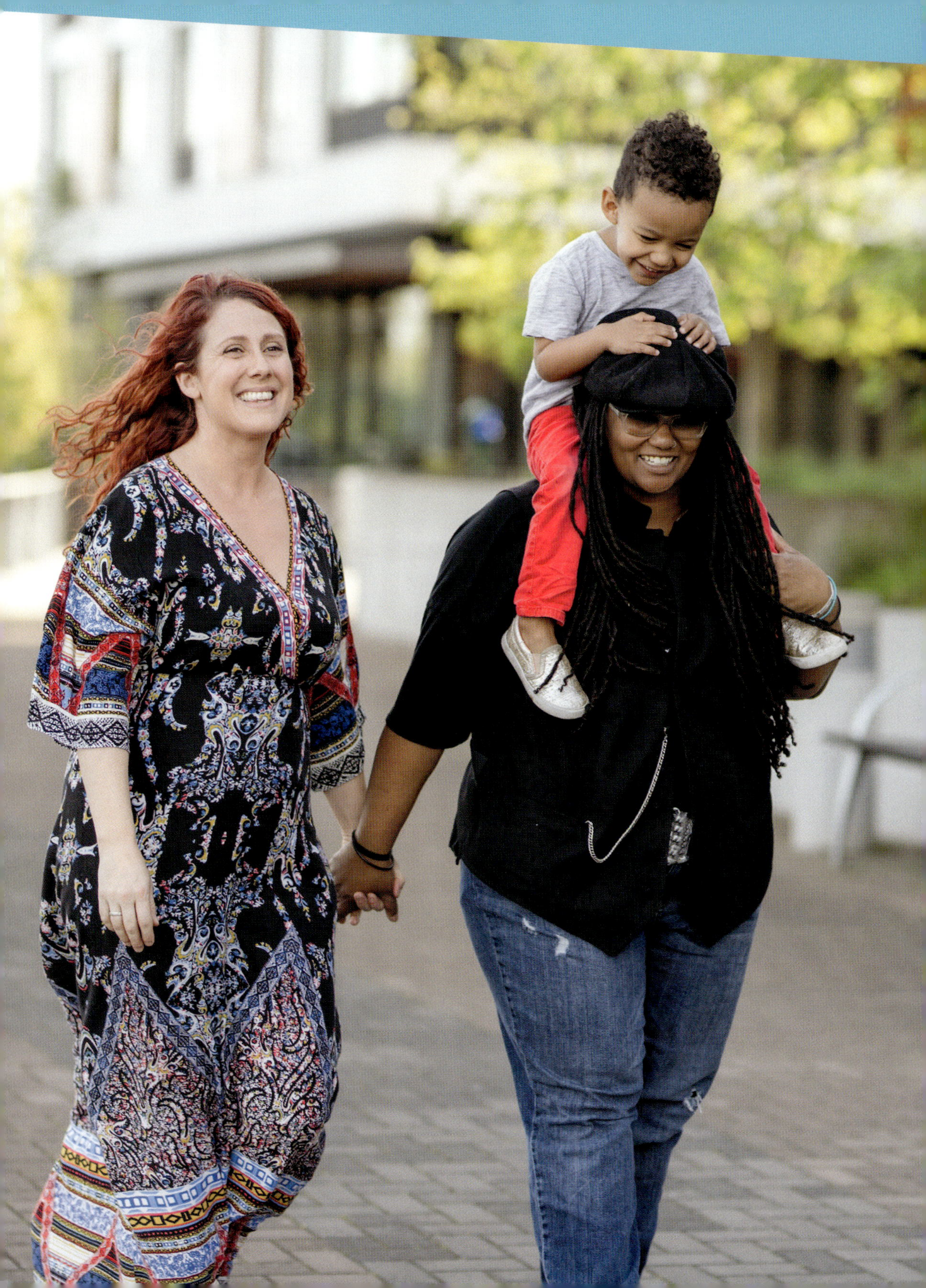

Chapter 2

Many Ways to Make a Family

Every child needs a family to love them and help them grow up. Some children are born into a family. Other children are adopted into a family.

> **Every year, approximately 135,000 children are adopted in the United States.**

Adoption happens when someone becomes the child of an adult who did not give birth to them. Sometimes **birth parents** cannot take care of a child. So sometimes, that child can be adopted. Parents who adopt want to love and care for a child who needs a family.

Some children are adopted as babies. Others are adopted when they are older. Some adopted children live with a mom and a dad. Others might live with only

> **Many babies are adopted within a month of being born.**

their mom or only their dad. Some children have two moms or dads.

Some adopted children live with their grandparents. Some children live with aunts and uncles. Others grow up in **blended families**.

Some children live in foster families. A **foster parent** takes care of the child. The child lives with them for a while. This might be for weeks, months, or years. Later, a foster child might return to their birth parents. Or they might be adopted by their foster family.

Did You Know?

National Adoption Day is in November. It is for foster children who are waiting to be adopted. It is also for all families that form through adoption.

Some children are not related to their foster parents. Other children are.

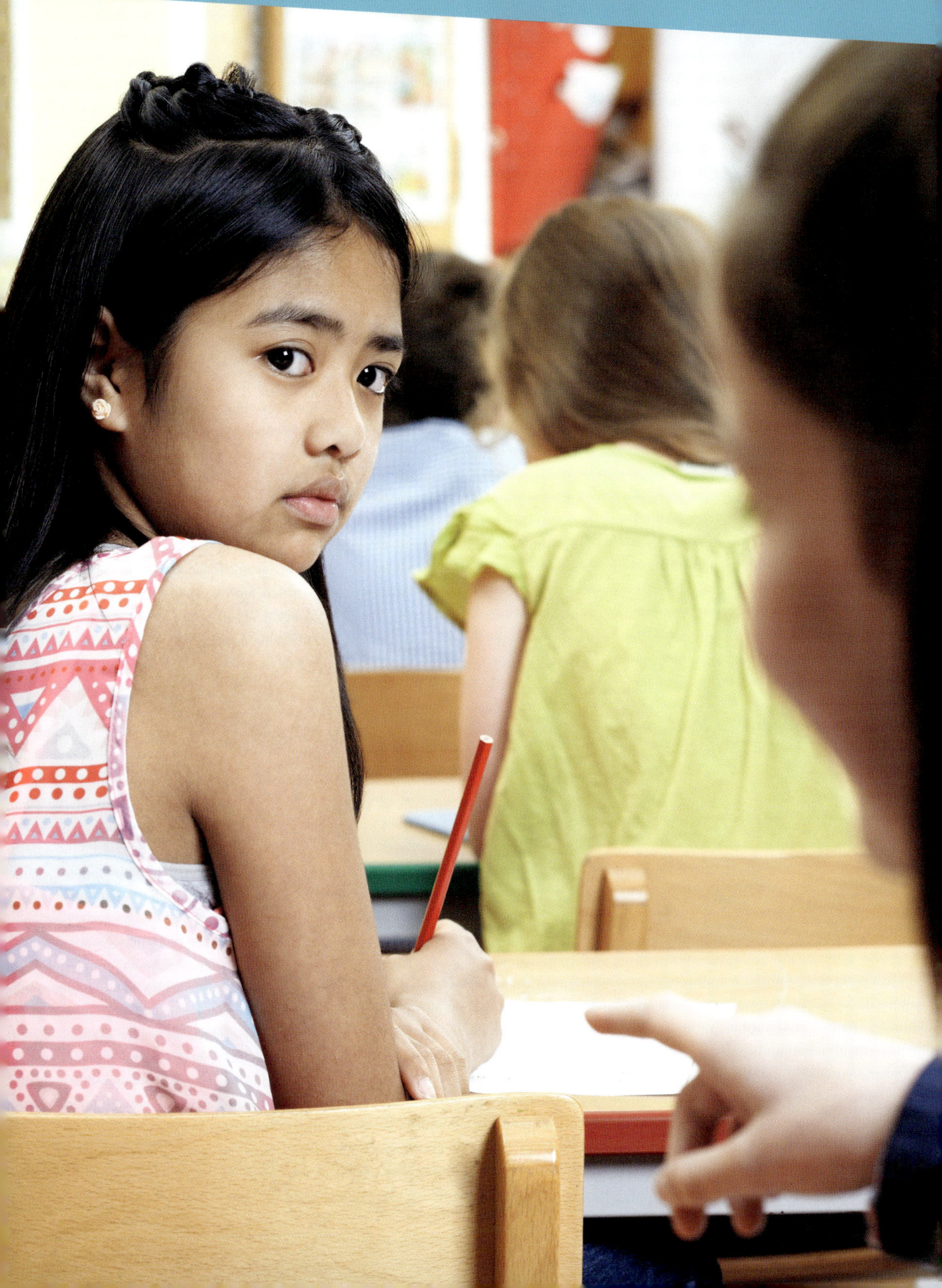

Chapter 3

Questions and Challenges

An **adoptee** may have experiences that other children do not have. For example, their family members might not look like one another. Family members might have different skin colors.

> Adoptees who look different from their parents can face bullying at school.

People outside of the family might ask, "Are those your real parents?" Or they might ask, "Is that your real sister?" People may not mean to hurt a child's feelings. But hearing these questions can still feel hurtful. A child could feel like they don't belong in their family.

However, adoptees do belong in their families. They belong as much as children born into the family. Parents love them as fully as they

▷ **It can take time to process strong feelings such as anger or sadness.**

love children who were born into the family.

Adoptees might also have important questions of their own.

Sometimes kids do not understand why they were adopted. They may want to know more about their birth family. They may wonder why they can't live with their birth family.

Some adoptees do not receive answers to these questions. But others are able to visit

Did You Know?

In the United States, 1 in 25 families has adopted a child. Half of those families have welcomed children both by adoption and by birth.

> Open adoptions have become more common over time.

members of their birth family.

When this happens, it is called an **open adoption**.

MANY IDENTITIES

All in One

Some families welcome children by both adoption and birth. Parents love all of their children in the same way. It doesn't matter how the children join the family. Sometimes, though, adoptees might feel less close to their families than their siblings do.

If this happens, members of these families can respond in many ways. For example, some parents encourage conversation. Family members can share their thoughts and feelings. Sharing can help people feel close to one another. This helps everyone feel like they belong in the family.

Sharing can create strong ties of love and friendship between children.

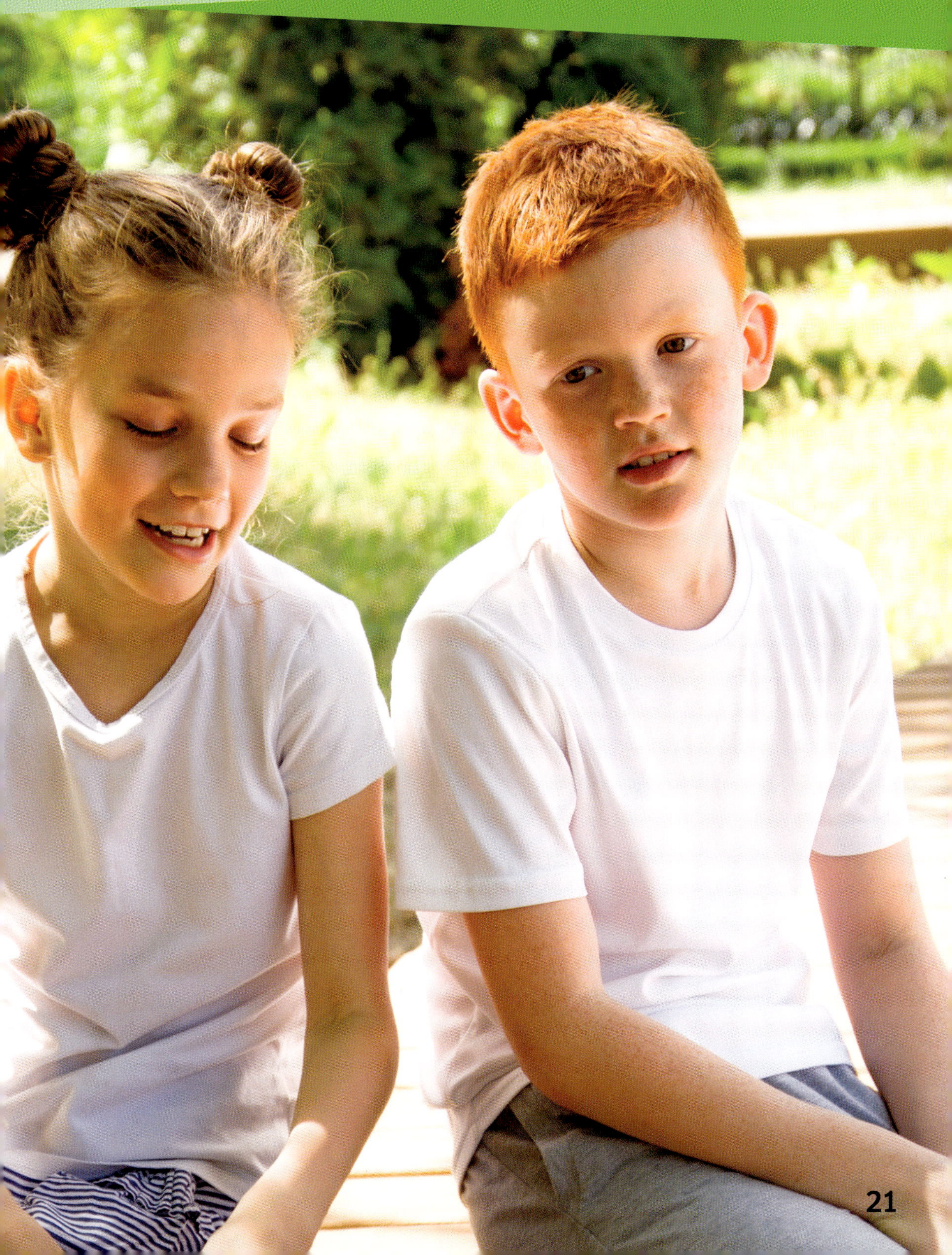

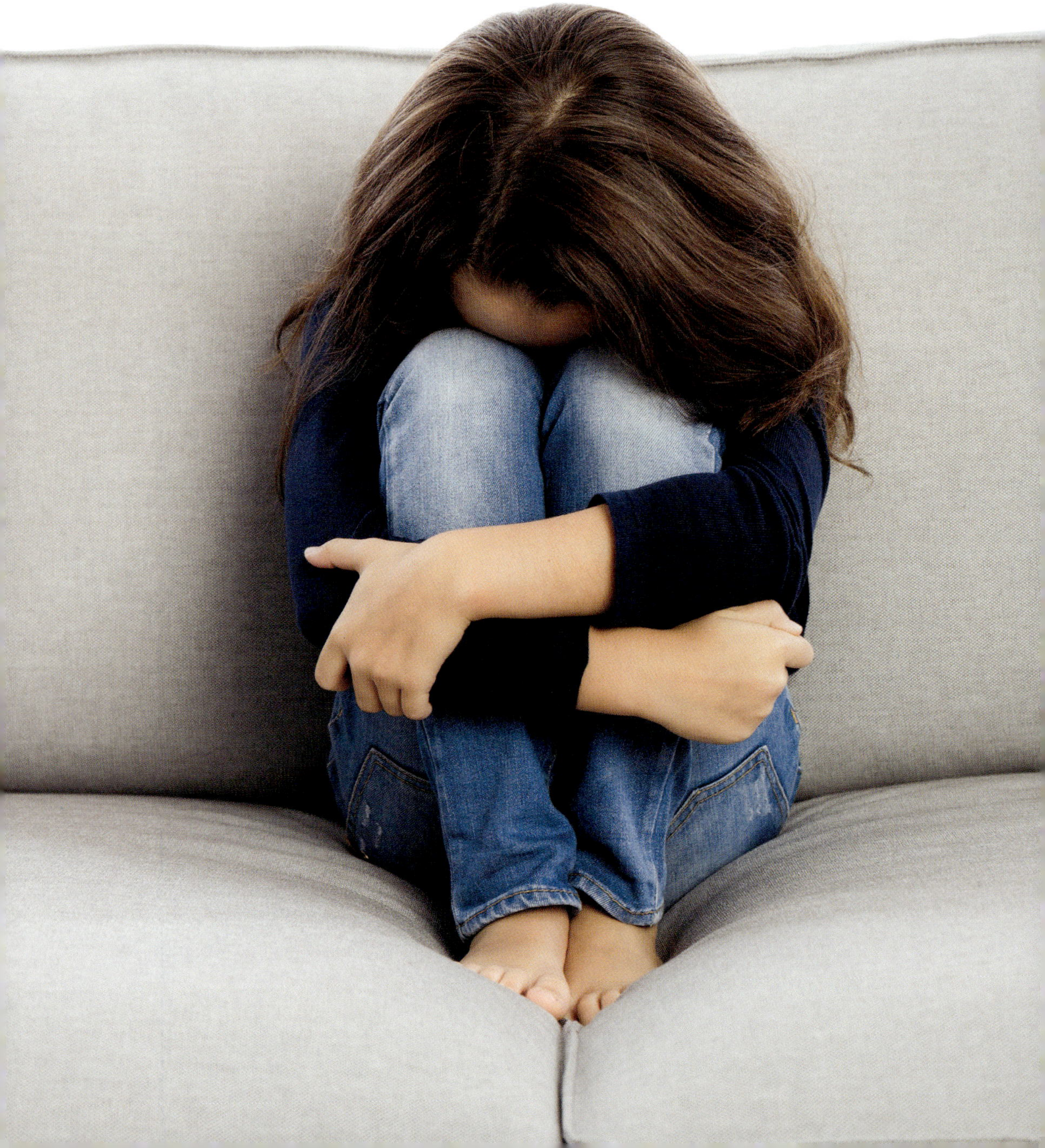

Chapter 4

Belonging

Adoption is always about two types of families. Adopted children have a birth family and an adoptive family. Adoptees do not live with their birth parents. They may feel sad, angry, or confused about this.

▶ **Strong emotions might not always feel good. But they are okay to have.**

Being adopted can also make children feel good and happy. They feel loved and safe when they belong to a family. In fact, children often have more than one feeling. That's because being adopted is complex.

Children might have questions about being adopted. This is common. An adoptee can share their thoughts with their parents. They can also talk to a good friend. Kids can talk to **counselors**, too.

> **With counselors, adoptees can use toys to share and explore their feelings.**

Sometimes, people have answers for adoptees. Other times, they might not. But they can still help adoptees work through feelings.

Children who are not adopted might have questions, too. They can talk to their parents or a teacher. Or they might be able to talk to an adoptee. They can ask **respectful** questions. That way, they can learn what it is like to be adopted.

Did You Know?

Nearly 100 million Americans have experience with adoption. Some are adoptees themselves. Others may have a family member or friend who was adopted.

> **Having a feeling of belonging can play an important role in growing up well.**

There are many ways to make a family. Adoption is one way that children find belonging.

FOCUS ON
Adoptive Families

Write your answers on a separate piece of paper.

1. Write a sentence summarizing the main ideas in Chapter 3.

2. Do you think it is important for adoptees to connect with their birth families? Why or why not?

3. In the United States, how many families have adopted a child?
    - A. 1 in 25 families
    - B. nearly 100 million families
    - C. all families

4. How can having a lifebook help an adoptee?
    - A. A lifebook contains details about a child's birth family and adoptive family.
    - B. A lifebook tells a made-up story.
    - C. A lifebook shows possible future families.

5. What does **experience** mean in this book?

*Nearly 100 million Americans have **experience** with adoption. Some are adoptees themselves.*

    A. not knowing about something
    B. living through something in real life
    C. thinking something is not possible

6. What does **complex** mean in this book?

*In fact, children often have more than one feeling. That's because being adopted is **complex**.*

    A. involving just one part or feeling
    B. involving many parts or feelings
    C. not happening in real life

Answer key on page 32.

Glossary

adoptee
A person who is adopted.

adoption court
The place where a judge allows parents to adopt a child into a family.

birth parents
The first parents of an adoptee.

blended families
Families that include children from earlier relationships.

counselors
People whose job is to listen and to help people work through problems.

foster parent
An adult who cares for a child for a limited amount of time.

open adoption
An adoption where a child has contact with members of the birth family.

respectful
Treating others with care for their feelings and happiness.

To Learn More

BOOKS

Cavell-Clarke, Steffi. *Different Families*. New York: Crabtree Publishing, 2019.

Hicks, Dwayne. *What's Life Like in Foster Care?* New York: PowerKids Press, 2019.

Wilkerson, Amy. *Being Adopted*. Meadville, PA: Fulton Books, 2021.

NOTE TO EDUCATORS

Visit **www.focusreaders.com** to find lesson plans, activities, links, and other resources related to this title.

Index

A
adoptee, 15–18, 20, 23–26
adoption court, 5

B
belonging, 16, 20, 24, 27
birth family, 7, 18–19, 23
birth parents, 10, 12, 23
blended families, 11

C
counselors, 24

E
experiences, 15, 26

F
feelings, 16, 20, 23–25
foster families, 12
friends, 24, 26

L
lifebook, 7
love, 5, 9–10, 16–17, 20, 24

N
National Adoption Day, 12

O
open adoption, 19

Q
questions, 16–18, 24, 26

S
sharing, 20, 24

Answer Key: **1.** Answers will vary; **2.** Answers will vary; **3.** A; **4.** A; **5.** B; **6.** B